More praise for *Nobody Is Ever Missing*:

'Catherine Lacey – with the ease of a master – depicts a mind that may, or may not, be breaking down . . . Page after page, the novel strikes those rarely accomplished balances between action and interiority, comedy and bleakness, stream-of-consciousness and clarity' *Time Out New York*

'Witty, knowing and lyrical' *Spectator*

'A serious, frequently brilliant novel with a sustained intensity that is rare in fiction. It's the most promising first novel that I've encountered this year' *Wall Street Journal*

'A beautiful, haunting literary novel that also happens to be a real page-turner . . . *Nobody Is Ever Missing* is a wonderful debut novel, reminiscent of Elena Ferrante or Amy Hempel, and Catherine Lacey is a serious talent' Jonathan Lee, author of *Joy*

'Catherine Lacey's voice is wholly unique, somehow managing to be both a challenge and a relief at the same time. *Nobody Is Ever Missing* is one of my favourite books of the year, a journey to the other side of the world I won't soon forget' Jami Attenberg, author of *The Middlesteins*

'Fierce, funny, haunting . . . Elyria may be adrift, but her observations are sharp and original' *Sunday Express*

'Like a cigarette packet, this disturbing but impressively sustained debut should carry a warning: read only if feeling robust. In long, looping sentences, Lacey enmeshes us in Elly's thoughts as they bash round in circles like trapped bees' *Intelligent Life*

NOBODY IS EVER MISSING

CATHERINE LACEY

GRANTA

Granta Publications, 12 Addison Avenue, London W11 4QR

First published in Great Britain as an ebook by Granta Books, 2014
Trade paperback edition published 2015
This paperback edition published 2016

First published in the United States by Farrar,
Straus and Giroux, New York, in 2014

A CIP catalogue record for this book is available from the
British Library.

1 3 5 7 9 10 8 6 4 2

ISBN 978 1 78378 089 1
eISBN 978 1 78378 088 4

Designed by Jonathan D. Lippincott

Offset by Avon DataSet Limited, Bidford on Avon

Printed and bound by CPI Group (UK) Ltd, Croydon, CR0 4YY

www.grantabooks.com

In memory of MG

There sat down, once, a thing on Henry's heart
só heavy, if he had a hundred years
& more, & weeping, sleepless, in all them time
Henry could not make good.
Starts again always in Henry's ears
the little cough somewhere, an odour, a chime.

And there is another thing he has in mind
like a grave Sienese face a thousand years
would fail to blur the still profiled reproach of.
    Ghastly,
with open eyes, he attends, blind.
All the bells say: too late. This is not for tears;
thinking.

But never did Henry, as he thought he did,
end anyone and hacks her body up
and hide the pieces, where they may be found.
He knows: he went over everyone, & nobody's
    missing.
Often he reckons, in the dawn, them up.
Nobody is ever missing.

—John Berryman, "Dream Song 29"

NOBODY IS EVER MISSING

1

There might be people in this world who can read minds against their will and if that kind of person exists I am pretty sure my husband is one of them. I think this because of what happened the week I knew I'd be leaving soon, but he didn't know; I knew I needed to tell him this but I couldn't imagine any possible way to get my mouth to make those words, and since my husband can unintentionally read minds, he drank a good deal more than usual that week, jars of gin mostly, but tall beers from the deli, too. He'd walk in sipping a can hidden in a paper bag, smile like it was a joke.

I would laugh.

He would laugh.

Inside our laughing we weren't really laughing.

The morning I left he got out of bed, got dressed, and left the room. I stayed cold awake under shut lids until I heard our front door close. I left the apartment at noon wearing my backpack and I felt so sick and absurd that I walked into a bar instead of the subway. I ordered a double bourbon even though I don't usually drink like that and the bartender asked me where

I was from and I said Germany for no good reason, or maybe just so he wouldn't try to talk to me, or maybe because I needed to live in some other story for a half hour: I was a lone German woman, here to see the Statue of Liberty and the Square of Time and the Park of Central (not a woman taking a one-way flight to a country where she only knew one person, who had only once extended an offer of his guest room, which, when she thought of it again, seemed to be the kind of invitation a person extends when they know it won't be taken but it was too late now because I was taking it and oh well oh well oh well).

A man took the stool beside me despite a long row of empties, ordered a cranberry and nothing.

What's your trouble? he asked me. *Tell me your trouble, baby.*

I looked back at him like I didn't have any trouble to tell because that's my trouble, I thought, not knowing how to tell it, and this is why my favorite thing about airport security is how you can cry the whole way through and they'll only try to figure out whether you'll blow up. They'll still search you if they want to search you. They'll still try to detect metal on you. They'll still yell about laptops and liquids and gels and shoes, and no one will ask what's wrong because everything is already wrong, and they won't look twice at you because they're only paid to look once. And for this, sometimes, some people are thankful.

2

They looked and made quick calculations: a 7 percent chance of con artistry, 4 percent chance of prostitution, 50 percent chance of mental instability, 20 percent chance of obnoxiousness, a 4 percent chance of violent behavior. I was probably none of these things, at least not at first, but to all the passing drivers and everyone else in this country I could be anything, so they just slowed, had a look, made a guess, kept driving.

Women—they'd squint quick, make a worried face, continue on. Men (I later learned) stared from the farthest distance—their eyes trained to stay on me in case I was something they needed to shoot or capture—but they hardly ever stopped. Up close, I was not so promising: just a woman wearing a backpack, a cardigan, green sneakers. And young-seeming, of course, because you must seem young to get away with this kind of vulnerability, standing on a road's shoulder, showing the pale underside of your arm. You must seem both totally harmless and able, if necessary, to push a knife through any tender gut.

But I didn't know any of this at first—I just stood

and waited, not knowing that wearing sunglasses would always leave me stranded, not knowing that wearing my hair down meant something I did not mean, not knowing that my posture had to be so carefully calibrated, that I should always stand like a dancer ready to leap.

All I knew was what I'd read on that map at the airport: south until I hit Wellington, across on the ferry, then Picton, Nelson, Takaka, and Golden Bay, Werner's farm, the address scrawled on that bit of paper that had started all this.

When the plane landed that morning, I hadn't slept for thirty-seven hours or so. After they'd dimmed the lights I'd kept my eyes wide, my brain cruising into an endless horizon. I didn't read anything or watch anything on the screen inches from my face. I listened to sleeping bodies breathe; I tried to pick words out of feathery voices, rows away. The flight attendants swayed down the aisles and winked and pursed their lips and handed me very certain amounts of food substance: bread roll smooth as a lightbulb; tongue-sized piece of chicken; thirty-two peanuts in a metallic pocket. I bit into a flap of cheese, not noticing the plastic, then gave up on food.

Outside baggage claim I watched a man smoking a cigarette and kicking something along the curb, sunlight splintering around him like a painting of a saint. This was all it was, this country I'd catapulted into.

Oh, how could I not stop for you? that first driver asked. *How could I not?*

I don't know, I said. *How could you?*

The woman laughed but I was not in a place to see humor. I suppose it had been funny, but when I stared back at her with nothing on my face she stopped laughing. A long, curved nose gave her the regal but unflattering look of a falcon or toucan. She spoke to me like I was a child, which was fine because I wanted to be one. Lately, I couldn't remember those years, as if childhood was a movie I'd only seen the previews to.

You're a brave lass, aren't you? Don't see many like you out on the road.

There's a certain kind of woman who will notice someone's terror and call it bravery.

I thought lots of people hitchhiked here.

Oh, not too many, she said. *Not anymore. Everywhere is dangerous these days. Would you have a pear? Help yourself to a Nashi. I have loads of 'em, a special at the grocery.*

She told me about her eleven-year-old son, an accident she'd made in her twenties, and I ate a pear with the juice going everywhere, but she was only going to Papakura, so she let me out by a petrol station not far down the highway.

Don't you let any blokes pick you up, you hear? If one stops, you just let him keep going. We're always keeping an eye out, other women, you know. Another will stop for you soon enough.

I said I would, but I knew I wouldn't take her advice, because I can never manage to reject anyone's offer of anything; this was one of the only things about myself of which I was certain.

For a while there were no cars to show my thumb to, but I kept standing there, not even having an appropriate curiosity about this new country (a boring little mountain, a plain blue lake, a gas station, the same as ours only slightly not). The skin on my lips was drying and I thought about how all the cells on every body are on their way to a total lack of moisture and everyone alive has that thought all the time but almost no one says it and no one says it because they don't really *think* that thought, they just have it, like they have toes, like most people have toes; and the knowledge that we're all drying up is what presses the gas pedal in all the cars people drive away from where they are, which reminded me that I wasn't going anywhere, and I noticed that many cars had passed but none had stopped or even slowed, and I began to wonder about what would happen if no one took me, if the first woman had been a fluke and hitchhiking had been left in the seventies with other now-dangerous things—lead paint, certain plastics, free love—and I was going to be stuck here forever, watching no cars drive by, thinking about my cells all helpless to their drying.

I decided to try to look happy because I thought someone might be more inclined to pick up someone who was happy.

I am happy, I told myself, *I am a happy person.*

I opened my eyes more than was necessary and hoped this would convey my happiness to the cars, but they kept passing.

One honked, as if to say, *No.*

My arm stayed out for a long time and my elbow

ached at the spot where they'd always taken the blood, and I became so accustomed to the passing cars that I forgot that the point of all this was for me to get into a car and go somewhere, but nothing was following anything else—one car would pass, then another, but all the cars came and went alone. And I was here. And nothing had followed me—I was a human non sequitur—senseless and misplaced, a bad joke, a joke with no place to land. The sky was a good sky color and the air was healthy feeling, and maybe this was the kind of day that reminded all those drivers that days are a finite resource and it's best to protect the ones you have. This kind of day doesn't want you to dare it, doesn't want you to flip a coin, doesn't want you to pick up a stranger off the side of the road.

But eventually that first woman was proven right—it was the women who stopped, who insisted they *never* picked up hitchhikers, only women with thumbs out, damsels in transportation distress—which was what the second woman said, and I thought, Sure, fine, whatever—I wasn't going to mince words with anyone. There was no reason for that. She was on her way home from a hospital where she was a nurse, so I asked her what I had been thinking about ever since that last day at the lab:

What do they do with the blood? After they're done with it, I mean.

What blood? she asked.

When they test it. After they test it for disease or hormone levels or whatever. All those tubes of it—what happens?

Well, they dispose of it. It is hazardous waste.

But where does it go?

Into a secure place. First a tube, then a hazardous-waste container, then the containers are taken away by a company. They put it somewhere safe and secure and no one ever touches it ever again.

And that put an end to our talking. We didn't say another thing until she let me out where she had to let me out.

Good luck, she said, *take care. And stay away from those blokes.*

3

It became clear after some hours of waiting on the narrow, tree-lined road where the nurse had let me out that some places are not good places to be a person and not a car and that was where I was; occasional cars sped around the road bend and I ended up frightening drivers the way that wild animals do when they stand stunned dumb in a road. The cars would slow or swerve or honk and I wished I could honk back—*I know, I know*—*why am I here?* It was also unclear to me. After a while a little red car made a three-point turn and pulled up beside me and he leaned over to pop open the passenger door and I got in and thought, this is exactly who they said I should stay away from and exactly what I am not staying away from, and the bloke said, *Where you headed?*, and I said, *The ferry*, and he said, *Which one?*

Um, to the South Island?

The South Island?

Yeah?

Well, you're a long ways off—where you coming from?

The airport?

I was saying everything like a question because everything was a question.

Yer all wop-wops, aren't ya, all the way out here in Ness Valley?

Someone left me here, I said, and wondered if the nurse hadn't liked talking about work, about blood. I couldn't remember if I had even told her where I was trying to go.

The bloke drove me back up the hills I'd come down with the nurse, past the petrol stations, the fields of sheep, the repeated green plants, the narrow roads turning into more little roads, and what was the point of it, I wondered, of all this world, these plants, these sheep, this place?

The most beautiful country in the world, the bloke said a few times, but I knew that lots of people tell themselves things like that but there is no country that is the most beautiful country. The bloke let me out where one road met another road. *Lots of cars*, he said, and there were lots of cars but none of them stopped for me. The sky went dark and this was not the kind of place where streetlights were, this was a bring-your-own-light kind of environment and I didn't have any light, hadn't brought any light, hadn't thought about how I'd need light. It was the first of many things I was unprepared for.

I saw a little shed on the edge of a field with a large hole ripped in it, so I crawled in, ran my hands along the inside looking for snakes or rats, but I just found a rusted-up hammer and a horseshoe and an empty glass bottle. It is best to sleep through the dark, I thought, so I am doing the best I can. As I fell asleep I thought that the appropriate feeling would have been fear or regret or some soup of both, but that wasn't what I felt; I reminded myself that once I got to Werner's farm my life would become small and manageable and wouldn't involve sleeping in sheds or hitchhiking, so I slept like I was already the simplest woman in the world.

The next morning I woke to an unfamiliar noise happening outside the shed and it reminded me of a familiar noise: Husband in the other room, his office, the rhythmic chalk clack, a pause, more clacking. There was something about the smell of it, the color of it, he said, that loosened up his brain, let the numbers fall out in the right order.

I thought you hated the chalkboard, I imagined him saying to my nostalgia.

I do, but the sound of you putting things on it makes it okay.

My husband, smiling in the back of my brain: I remembered him this way.

I rolled up my makeshift bed, folded the towel and T-shirt back into my pack, and climbed out of the hole to find that the unfamiliar noise was sheep swishing in the grass, but the sheep stampeded away because sheep are smart enough not to trust anyone for anything, especially not people who sleep in and crawl out of sheds, and I couldn't disagree with those sheep because I would run away from me, too, if I was a sheep and not me and even if I was me, I'd still like, some mornings, to be the thing running far from me instead of sewn inside myself forever.

•

I heard an engine behind me as I was walking down a road's shoulder, so I stuck my arm out but when I turned around I was surprised to see a school bus; it hadn't sounded that large. I pulled my arm in, stepped farther away from the road, thinking it wouldn't be right to get a ride from a bus if it was full of kids, to expose young lives to me since I wasn't yet convinced that I wasn't a form of radiation. But the bus stopped and the driver cranked open the door.

It's not safe here. Get in.

No, it's okay. I should just wait on a regular car.

Nah, nah, nah, get on in.

Are you sure?

I'll just take you up the road where it's safer. Can't have you out here on this part of the road. Too dangerous. It's not right.

I found an open seat and a pigtailed girl leaned across the aisle to say, *I'm ten*, and I wasn't sure what to say, so I said, *I'm twenty-eight*, not quite thinking.

You're not twenty-eight, a girl with red hair said, laughing as if I had claimed to be an elephant.

I'm not?

Noooo.

How old do you think I am?

A hundred, pigtails said.

No, she's not! She's probably fifteen because my sister is sixteen and she's bigger than her.

What are you really? pigtails asked.

I forget, I said.

Where are you going? the redhead asked.

I don't know. To a farm somewhere.

Are you a farmer?

Sure, I said.

Where's your farm?

I pointed south, or I think I pointed south, but I could have pointed west, or even north, and what would it matter? If you made enough turns it would take you to the same place. The girls in the back were chanting something and slapping their hands together with increasing speed and volume.

Quiet back there, the driver yelled, and so they were.

The redhead leaned around the edge of my seat and put her face near my elbow. She had skin the texture of cheap toilet paper and luminous green eyes, little luxury items planted in her skull. The bones in her face were more pronounced than you'd expect on a girl her age —either underfed or a natural look of vulnerability.

Can I tell you a secret? she whispered. *We're runaways. We all run away from our homes. He's taking us to the police.*

I peeked over my shoulder at the other girls. A few leaned their swan necks into the aisle looking toward me. I could hear some high voices dipping low to whisper.

What's your name?

Elyria. What's yours?

Alison. Where are you from?

New York. Where are you from?

A different planet. I ran away from outer space. Nebulas don't interest me. She smiled with all her tiny teeth. *You want to know another secret?*

Sure.

I have two hearts. A regular one and a little baby one underneath it. And you know what else? I have a third eyeball stuck in my brain but it can't see anything because it's too dark in there. That's what the doctor told me. He showed me a picture of it they took in a big white room with a robot. Have you ever seen a robot? Because I have.

Her face had pinched into something serious, and I didn't know what to say and I couldn't tell if she was telling the truth about the robot, the doctor, the extra eye, the extra heart—what a terrible thing to have too many of—but the bus stopped and the bus driver put his arm up and waved me forward.

Bye, I said.

See you later, Alison said.

When I got to the front of the bus the driver was just staring forward, and I looked at his gnarled hands ten-and-two-ing and I saw how the flesh hung on his face like it was clay pressed on in a rush, all uneven and loose, and something in his jaw clench and nostril flare made me worry he was doing something with his life that was bloody, something that involved heads pressed against concrete or mouths filled with something that shouldn't be there and I wondered if this was true and if it was true I knew he would continue to plow over life, continue to chop lives like a tractor, and he would keep doing that forever unless I killed him right here with my bare hands in front of all the girls, then threw his corpse out the door and drove these girls straight to the hospital for post-traumatic stress treatment, and though I knew I had the potential to do this locked in me like a poisonous pet snake, I knew I didn't have the part of a person you must have to turn that potential kinetic, to be the kind of person who can let their awful plow.

Thanks, I said to the bus driver, to cover up what I was thinking, and one of the girls in the back shouted, *Takes one to know one*, and it made me gasp even though I knew she wasn't talking to me and I worried that what I had seen in the driver was something I'd seen in myself, that it took me to know me.

The bus driver said, *You're welcome*, and I wondered if he knew what else I was.

4

I walked roadside for a few hours, wondering if it was possible that Alison really did have an extra eye, an extra heart, if a person could ever live with that kind of surplus, and something about the way Alison spoke reminded me of how Ruby spoke, or how Ruby said something once about having two hearts. Or maybe I was misremembering some more complicated thing Ruby said, something that made it clear we didn't speak the same language, that we couldn't fully translate ourselves to each other. There was a night I realized this, how we could no longer or perhaps had never quite been able to hear each other—

Who lets a sixteen-year-old move to New York alone?

We were smoking cigarettes in the backyard after a late Thanksgiving dinner (Mom's cigarettes, of course, the *who* to her question) and I didn't know whether I should ask her about college life as a child prodigy— Was she lonely? Had she made friends? Were her classes, finally, challenging enough? I knew I wouldn't understand her answers to those questions, that she'd allude to philosophical concepts I'd never heard of, that she'd make references I couldn't place and I'd just stare, baffled and unable to keep up. I was barely passing the high school classes she'd been exempt from.

As we smoked I pushed Ruby on the swing set, and we could see Mom passed out and drooling on a love seat in the sunroom. She'd been at a fever pitch all day, swigging Beaujolais, burning all the takeout in a reheating attempt, calling Ruby the *renegade genius* and accidentally ashing onto her plate.

There's our little genius, our little renegade teenage genius! How does she do it? I just don't know how she does it!

But finally everything was quiet, just the swing creak and our faint exhalations and even though this was one of the thousands of chances I had to have a meaningful talk with Ruby, something sisterly and emotional, I didn't take that chance: I stilled the swing and held out an imaginary microphone to her: *Tell us, Ruby, how do you do it?*

And Ruby ran with it because she also wanted to live in a fiction, to keep playing pretend.

Well, I'll tell ya, Bob. The secret of my success is to make a plan and act fast. I don't second-guess myself. I'm never of two minds about anything.

Well, folks, there you have it, I said, but there were no folks.

A van slowed and stilled beside me and this memory sank away. The driver leaned out his window, his right arm was covered in tattoos, matte-black vines blurring into dark skin.

Simon, he said.

Elyria, I said.

Elyria! That's a helluva name. Hippie parents?

Not really.

I didn't tell him, like I didn't tell anyone, that Elyria was a town in Ohio that my mother had never visited. That was all my name meant: a place she'd never been.

The basic idea of a mustache was hanging over Simon's mouth, and there were these odd wrinkles around his eyes that didn't agree with the rest of his machine-smooth face.

I stared at the pointless hills rippling around us— the trees all captive to the ground, a grey mountain in the distance, stoic and bored—and Simon started a monologue on himself, his autobiography—

Been traveling for seven months on the North Island, did some wine work for a while to save money, but I've been on my own for a long time. I separated from my parents when I was sixteen. My father clobbered the shit out of my little brother one night, put him in the hospital, and I said . . . you know . . . check, please? All done with this, thanks. Ever seen a ten-year-old with a black eye from his own pops? It's not something you want to ever see.

I almost liked how much he talked, how he answered his own questions, how simple it all was, like television. I hadn't said more than ten words and maybe those were the last words I was ever going to say for the rest of my life, I thought, as Simon went on about how his parents were put in jail, something to do with fraud, with some kind of real estate scheme, houses in Miami, London, L.A., all confiscated, and maybe this was it—this was all I needed—someone who just naturally filled in all the silence that life has in it.

Pops tried to blame it on me and even the judge knew he was pulling a porky. My pop had a stink-eye. Anyone with half a thought in his head could see it. It was in the news then, tabloid shit mostly. You know, Tattooed Teen Divorces Parents—Violence Alleged—that kind of shit.

He let himself laugh weakly.

That's terrible, I said, stepping out of my silence.

Is what it is.

People say that when they mean something is terrible.

You're right. It is terrible.

5

Another terrible thing was how I met my husband.

He was wearing a suit that day and his deep red tie made his eyes seem even greener and brought out the pale pink in his face. He was thirty-two, but still looked boyish. I was barely twenty-two but everyone guessed older. We were sitting in a small and brutally lit waiting area in the university police office. We sat next to each other for maybe twenty minutes without saying anything and we didn't even bend a glance at the other because it's hard to do that when you're thinking about what a woman can do to herself and how a brick courtyard on a nice autumn afternoon can so quickly become a place you'll never want to see again. Police officers were speaking into phones and walkie-talkies and one of them walked over to ask me my name.

Elyria Marcus.

Ruby was your sister?

Adopted, yeah, I said, in case they knew that she had been Korean and could see from looking at me that I wasn't.

The officer nodded and made a note on her clipboard. She looked at my husband, who was just a stranger sitting next to me at that point and it hadn't yet crossed my mind to wonder why he was there or who he might be.

Professor, we need to ask you a few questions if you don't mind, she said.

Of course, he said, following her to the back of the office.

While he was gone Mother showed up, limp and sleepy on whatever Dad was slipping her those days. Dad wasn't there of course; he was still in Puerto Rico doing cheap boob jobs or something. Mom fell into the seat beside me.

Oh, it's waaarm, she slurred. *What a nice surprise.*

She snaked her arm around mine and put her head on my shoulder.

Baby, baby, my little baby. It's just you and me now. No more Ruby ring, Ruby slippers, Ruby Tuesday. Oh, our Ruby, Ruby.

It's normal, I've heard, for people to talk a little nonsense at times like these, but she wasn't even crying or seeming close to crying, which made me feel worse because I wasn't either. I tried to seem like I was in shock, but I wasn't, not really. Mother didn't even try to pretend she was in shock because that's the kind of beast she is. An officer came over to offer condolences or have her sign something, and she offered him her hand like she expected him to kiss it. He shook it with a bent wrist, then slipped away.

My precious little Ruby . . . What was it she always said, Elyria? Am I your favorite Asian daughter? Elly, you

*know she was my only Asian daughter. What on earth do
you think she meant by that? I never understood it. Was
that just a joke? Did she ever tell you what she meant?*

I wiped a smudge of lipstick off my mother's nose.
It looked like she had put it on while talking and driving, which was probably true.

It was a joke, Mom.

*Elyria, she was so beautiful, so smart. People must
have wondered how she could stand us. People must have
wondered, even I wondered. I stayed up late some nights
just watching her sleep, wondering how she'd ever be able
to stand it. I guess she just couldn't take it anymore, our
ugliness.*

Mom, stop.

*It's not our fault. We were just born like this. Well, not
really you, dear, but—*

She sat up, pushed her hair out of her face, and took
a lot of air into her body. She let it out slow, grabbed
my hand, looked me in the eye, and squeezed. It was
the first tender moment we'd had in years, but it ended
quickly.

I need so many cigarettes, she said, staggering away.
Through the glass wall in the front of the police office
I saw her light what would become the first of a dozen.
Every few minutes someone would approach her, almost bowing, it seemed. *Excuse me*, I could see their
mouths say, pointing to the NO SMOKING WITHIN 50 FT
OF THIS DOOR sign, and she would cut them off with a
shout I could hear through the glass. *Have you heard
of my daughter Ruby? Ruby Marcus? She died today and it
wasn't from secondhand smoke.* If that didn't work she
added, *Fuck off, I'm grieving*, which usually did.

The professor who wasn't yet my husband came back and stopped in front of me, standing a few inches too close and looking down. His paleness was glowing. I noticed his suit was too big around the middle and the sleeves too short.

Do you want to know anything? About her? I was the last one who spoke with her. That's what they think.

I didn't particularly care what some professor had said to Ruby. I'd seen her that morning; she was no mystery. We stood outside the library with paper cups of burnt coffee. She looked terrible, like she hadn't slept in days, and she said she felt even worse and I asked, *How much worse?*, and she said she didn't want to talk about it and I wasn't going to talk about it if she wasn't so we didn't talk about anything. We finished our coffees and walked in opposite directions. The blame (or at least some of it) was on me. I'd never figured out how to be related to her.

I didn't want to talk to anyone, and especially not about Ruby, but the professor's voice was so very level and calm. He sounded like some kind of radio reporter and I wanted to listen to this personal radio; I wanted his voice to play and play. Mother was lighting another cigarette outside, leaning against the glass, a dark bra visible through her wrinkled oxford.

Okay, I told the professor. *I'll listen.*

He sat down slowly, his knees angled toward me a little.

I'd only known Ruby since the semester started, when she became my TA. I knew she was overqualified, of course. She was talented, you know, and had been working on some incredible proofs.

His sentences were hard and plain, like he had been polishing them all afternoon.

I never understood what she did here, I said. We never talked about it.

Well . . . I don't know how to describe it, what Ruby seemed like today. I suppose I have a hard time reading faces, emotions, you know, the descriptive stuff. I'm more of a numbers person. But she seemed, just—maybe a little distracted. She gave me some papers she'd been working on. She said she wanted me to check them over, and she left.

What was it?

What do you mean?

The papers. Was it something important?

Um, no, not really. Something most grad students could do. She was capable of so much more than that. She'd been working on some very interesting stuff lately.

Oh.

I'm sorry.

No, it's fine. I mean, it doesn't matter that it was just regular stuff.

No, I mean, the whole thing. That she—

And I wished right then that I could gently cry, just cry—politely, humanly. Outside, my mother was screaming at someone, her breath making tiny smoke and steam clouds.

Thank you, I said to the professor.

He nodded, put his hands on his knees, leaned back a little, then leaned forward again. He looked at my mother, who was still screaming, then he looked at his feet.

When I was twenty my mother did it the same way as Ruby and, I just, well . . . today I've been thinking about it a lot, you know. Probably the most since it happened.

I didn't say anything. Mother was lighting one cigarette with another. A section of her hair was pushed over her head the wrong way. She turned around and waved at me with one limp, little hand, a royal dismissal. Lipstick rimmed her mouth like ice cream on a toddler.

I'm sorry for that, he said, *for saying that. I know it's what people always do, try to tell you they've already dealt with what you're dealing with, trying to tell you how they grieved—I know it doesn't help. I'm sorry. It was just on my mind.*

You don't need to be sorry, I said.

We didn't say anything for a little while.

He put his hand on my shoulder as if he was taking someone's advice to do so and he let it stay there for a moment and after that moment water did come out of my eyes and I felt more appropriate and more human to myself. The professor put his arms around me and I collapsed a little, making a wet spot on his navy jacket.

6

Exactly, Simon said, and he smiled and I knew that smile, and I remembered when I smiled like that at boys who smiled like that, but I hadn't seen that smile in at least seven years, and I'd never known my husband when he was young enough to let a gesture reveal himself so plainly. We had stopped for a sandwich and Simon was still filling up all the silence, and I did not smile back at him. I was no longer listening—most of my attention was on a man strumming a ukulele at the other end of the bar. A woman was looking at a menu and trying to get the man's attention, but he had his eyes closed. The woman waved her hands in front of the ukulele man's face but he just kept whistling, swaying. I looked back at Simon and copied his expression—serious, but with raised eyebrows—to make him think I was listening. Maybe he was too young to catch that trick. Maybe in the world of a twenty-one-year-old boy, no one had to fake an interest in you. The woman took away the man's ukulele. He looked, dejected, at the menu.

Here's something that may or may not be right in front of your face, Simon said, *you know, in front of your face in the sense that you already know it.*

Simon held my shoulders with both his hands, which felt larger and denser than I would have expected.

This is important—you and I, right now. This is important.

How's that? I said.

What's between people is more important than anything in the physical world. This is God, Elyria. Anytime two people can look at each other and talk honestly, that is God.

I wondered for a moment if he was trying to get me to join a cult, but I realized it was just his youth talking, not a dogma. I hadn't spoken much to Simon and what I'd said wasn't any kind of honesty, but Simon had perfected the art of seeing what he wanted to see, because it's easier to go through life like that, to see the world as a series of familiar things, a place where everyone feels how you feel and sees what you see. I was still impersonating Simon to his face to get away with ignoring him, and that seemed almost sustainable, a way to spend a few weeks, but when he went to the bathroom I went out to his unlocked van and strapped on my backpack and started walking somewhere even though Simon had told me he'd pitch a tent outside tonight and let me lock myself inside his van—*To prove a point,* he said, *I'm not a bad guy and I trust you*—but I didn't want to bear Simon anymore and I didn't want to be the thing under those projections anymore because I did have somewhere to go, in a way—Werner's farm, a place to sink into and forget about movement, about vibrations, about projections, about relying on whoever happened to pity me at that particular moment, increasingly disheveled, smelling more and more like the earth or an animal, caring less and less about how little I cared.

I walked through a forest near a highway until I found a clump of moss to sleep on and I remembered that Simon said possums were not indigenous to New Zealand, that they had been brought here by somebody a long time ago, some European, and since there were no animals here that liked to kill possums, all those unkilled possums *had fucked up the whole fucking ecosystem* by eating plants, too many plants, by wanting so much, and now there were *what?—ten or fifteen possums per person in New Zealand? Something fucked-up like that*; and I imagined my dozen fucked-up possums gathered around me, a personal audience, and I wondered which things inside a person might be indigenous or nonindigenous, but it isn't as easy to trace those kinds of things in a person as it is in a country. I wished that I could point to some colonizer and blame him for everything that was nonindigenous in me, whoever or whatever had fucked my ecosystem, had made me misunderstand myself—but I couldn't blame anyone for what was in me, because I am, like everyone, populated entirely by myself, which made me think, again, of Ruby on that Thanksgiving night on the swings, or maybe it was another night like that night when she was talking, I thought, about how predictable she felt—*I'm Asian so I'm supposed to be good at math and skip grades and I did and I'm adopted so I'm supposed to be messed up and I am*—and I tried to tell her she wasn't predictable, she wasn't a cliché, she wasn't a statistic—*You're a person, Ruby, like every-one else*—

Oh, thanks, she said, *like I really want to be like every-one else, Elyria, you're totally missing the point. I'm talking about free will*—and she went on for a long while making multitiered arguments about free will and the possibility that none of us had it. I was sixteen or seventeen and didn't have the kind of brain that Ruby had and this was becoming increasingly obvious, that my brain couldn't absorb as much as her brain could, that I couldn't expound with her about free will, that I was making a C in French and failing algebra and she had mastered both those classes during weekends one summer, and now here we were, she a teenage adult and me a teenage child and she wanted to talk about free will and I didn't have anything to say.

This was probably the moment she turned from my sister to an orphan again, and maybe I understood this then or maybe I understood this some weeks or years later, but Ruby and I were no longer two children together in an alternate universe, equally mystified by our parents and the whole world—we were now in separate alternate universes and from then on we only had rare moments where it seemed, for a second, there was some sense between us. Like that afternoon I admitted to her I'd come to Barnard so I could see her more often, and that other night when I talked her off—and I don't want to say ledge, but it was a ledge, of sorts, a metaphorical ledge—that night I talked her off a metaphorical ledge before her college graduation because she hated how it had taken her all four years to complete a triple major—but those sweet and connected moments between us became increasingly rare, or else I have forgotten some or many of those moments, which is probably true because memories are so often made by one hand and deleted by the other, and living is a long churn of making and deleting and we all forget so much of what we could be remembering, and part of the deal with remembering those connected moments with Ruby was that they usually came with a more difficult memory, like the one from that Christmas—it must have been the one just after that Thanksgiving when we smoked on the swings. There was an evening that the three of us were somehow all sitting in the breakfast room drinking hot cocoa as if imitating some more wholesome family and even Mother had been doing a pretty good job at playing the part of the mother (she'd made the cocoa, had wrapped a present or two, and sincerely told Ruby she had missed her) but then she somehow dropped or threw her cup of cocoa and the spill seemed to inspire something in her, so she wordlessly pushed a box of ornaments from the table and left the room. Ruby and I swept up the shattered shards and sopped up the warm, dark mess and smiled at each other over this warm, dark mess but much later that night, when we found Mother shouting, *Open me! Open me!*, from inside a large cardboard box she'd taped up from the inside, we were all done with being amused, so we didn't smile at all. I'm the child of a child, I thought, and I may have said that to Ruby and she may have laughed, or maybe I didn't speak that thought at all. Eventually Mother got quiet and began snoring and we didn't bother to open that box because we knew how much she hated to be woken up.

Ruby turned on the TV and the first thing we saw was the title screen for *It's a Wonderful Life*. We looked at each other like *Yeah, uh-huh, sure*, and we ate cheese and crackers for dinner and watched that movie and we didn't have to talk because we knew what the other was thinking—this was one of those you-don't-have-to-say-it, I-suffer-like-you-suffer moments and our brains were calm and still, just lying there in our heads and our mother was also calm and still, just lying there in that box.

All three of us, I thought, all three of us are orphans.

7

I just write the soap opera and that's all and that's enough,
I told Harriet.

This was the afternoon she'd called to say I needed
to meet her in Union Square so she could introduce
me to Werner at his reading. I could have given a thousand reasons why I didn't want to go (that I had no interest in being whatever she thought a *real writer* was,
that I hated poetry, that I hated when people enjoyed
or pretended to enjoy poetry, that being around Harriet gave me the same tangled feeling I had while
watching television shows about sharks) but it wouldn't
have mattered—when Harriet made a decision, she
would practically burn down a forest to make sure it
happened.

You're wasting your good years, she said. *All that time
you've spent writing for other people, you could be putting
that energy into your own work. Tell your husband you're
quitting, that you need a year to write for yourself. You
know he'll be fine with it.*

She'd somehow read the story of mine that had
been published many years ago in a literary journal a
professor at Barnard had submitted it to without my

permission, and she tracked down my email to say she was an editor and interested in my novel, as if everyone had one. I told her I didn't have one and didn't want one, that I was a staff writer for a soap opera, but Harriet is the kind of person who believes you can frighten genius out of a person and be thanked for finding it.

How could that possibly ever be enough for you? You're a real writer, not a soap opera writer.

How was I supposed to feel about this? Because I was, in fact, a soap opera writer, and I was paid to do this and people followed the stories as if they were truth and those exaggerated lives were more real to some than anything actually real, so much so that whole magazines were devoted to this collective imagination. It had started as an in-between job, just a writer's assistant, but when one of the producers impulsively fired half the staff, I was promoted and I began to enjoy how nothing was recognizable or familiar about the love triangles, rectangles, and octagons, the operatic scream-crying, the scorned lovers, double homicides, sudden, rare illnesses, demonic curses, and all brands of revenge. Ruby had always described it best: *It's how we outsource rage.*

I don't want to feel literary, I told Harriet. *I just want to feel useful.*

Listen, you'll thank me for this later, believe me. I really do think that meeting Werner will be good for you. He always knows the right thing to say to a writer just starting out.

Harriet, I'm not starting anything. I don't want to write a book.

I'm sure that will change, she said, and I wanted to say that it wouldn't but she said, *I'll see you at six-thirty*, and I am not the kind of person who can put myself between a person and her wants.

In Harriet's introduction she said something about how Werner's poetry was the invention of a radical loneliness, a reinvention of life as we know it, and that was ridiculous, I knew, but who wouldn't want life to be reinvented? I thought everyone would like that very much. Werner's work was taught in universities, anthologized, published in magazines, and even reviewed in newspapers. Novelists and filmmakers cited him as a major influence and Mother even told me his poems made her cry for the first time in years, but I'd only read a poem or two and didn't even try to try to like it.

Once the reading was done, Harriet beelined to Werner, my wrist in her hand. She gave Werner a quick appraisal of the reading as he shrugged and said something lost to the din of the crowd.

This is Elyria. She's writing a very impressive novel.

Well, if it's impressive in its unfinished state it must be doubly impressive upon completion.

His accent—half-German, half-Kiwi—sounded like it belonged to some long-past century.

I'm certain it will be, Harriet said just as someone else caught her attention, and she was lost to a churn of people. Werner looked at me like he was waiting on some kind of explanation.

I'm not writing a novel, I said. *I don't like novels.*

It's for the best, Werner said. *Misery begins in publishing.*

And I am not what a person would call outspoken and I'm not even much of a speaker, according to some, and I don't know if it was because of how old and harmless Werner seemed or because I recognized something in him that gave me an odd comfort, but I spoke with a strange confidence, even a kind of arrogance, as if I was picking up arrogance from Werner like radio waves.

Well, that's a funny thing to say after all that publishing has gotten you, isn't it?

Is it?

I don't know.

Maybe misery begins everywhere, he said.

Behind me I could hear Harriet talking about Werner's brilliance. In front of me I could see Werner not even giving a shit.

I'd still rather be back in New Zealand away from this concrete wasps' nest. People in large quantities are terrible.

The fluorescents buzzed. The people buzzed.

I've always wanted to go to New Zealand, I said (then thought, I have?).

Well, if you do, you'll have a place to stay. I have an extra room on the farm.

Oh, I said, and the crowd parted us, left me with this idea.

Later that night, drinking gin with all of Harriet's people in her office, I asked Werner if he'd meant it, if he was really offering me a place to stay or if he was just being nice.

I'm not nice, he said, *and I don't pretend to be. I have an extra room. I'm not much good for company, but the room is yours if you want. You can tend the garden and we'll call it even.*

And though he sounded sincere I still suspected that this was one of those things a person says on impulse and then aggressively defends to mask the mistake.

Blank eyed, he scrawled an address on a bit of paper.

8

Only two cars and fifteen minutes passed before some-one stopped, a black truck driven by a sun-wrinkled lady wearing a straw hat.

Into town? she asked, and I took this as a chance to not make a decision, to just agree.

While we drove she asked me about myself and I found it impossible to answer anything honestly. She asked what had brought me to New Zealand and I said that my husband had. She asked me what my husband did and I said he was a farmer.

Well, he wants to be a farmer, I said. *That's why he's here.*

Everything grows here, the old woman said proudly. *All sorts of plants and other things. Do you have children?*

I laughed by accident, the kind of laugh that didn't say you thought something was funny.

No.

Well, my goodness. I suppose women really are putting off having children these days. You ought to get to it. I only bring it up because there is no joy in life greater than an empty house. Don't let the other women fool you with this empty-nest-syndrome stuff. Life gets better once the kids are out and the sooner you have them the sooner they can leave.

Ah. Okay, I said.

What's even better is finally being a widow.

The woman started laughing and laughing and laughing so much I felt like I had to laugh, too, so I did and then I realized we were laughing at how her husband was dead, which really didn't seem so funny, and I think we realized that at the same time, and we both stopped laughing and there was that deeply quiet moment after two people have laughed too much and we let that quiet moment stay for the rest of the drive. During that silence I thought of that night when my husband and I were having one of the arguments about the way we argue and I went into the kitchen to get a glass of water but instead picked up a knife because I was thinking about stabbing myself in the face—not actually considering stabbing myself in the face, but thinking that it would be a physical expression of how I felt—and I picked up a chef's knife, our heavy good one that I used for everything from cutting soft fruit to impaling pumpkins and I looked at it, laughed a noiseless laugh, put the chef's knife down, poured myself a glass of water, and drank it fast, until I choked a little, and I went back to arguing with my husband and he didn't know about my face-stabbing thoughts and it made me even angrier that he didn't know about my face-stabbing thoughts, that he couldn't just intuit these things, look into my eyes and know that the way he spoke to me was a plain waste of our life—but here in the car with the widowed stranger I didn't have to feel any of those feelings anymore because I had left my husband and our arguments and my chef's knife and I had come to this country where I could laugh, so gently, gently laugh at things that were actually not funny.

9

There was that night that my husband had looked at me like he wasn't sure if we knew each other or not, like we had met at a party years ago and now that we'd come across each other in the cereal aisle, he couldn't quite remember who I was. This look probably had something to do with the fact that I was crying and he hadn't seen me do that since the afternoon we met and that one time on our honeymoon. But this wasn't like that—this was six-thirty on a weeknight, aisles packed with clicking heels and crumpled suits.

He said, *Wheaties?*, and I opened my mouth to say it didn't matter, but had started sobbing instead.

Elly . . . what are you doing? Elly . . . Elyria . . .

He stood close, shielding me from other people's eyes, and I was happy he didn't try to touch me because that would have made it worse.

Elyria . . . ?

It's just—nothing—I just—I think I'm tired.

You're tired?

Isn't that okay? Am I not a person? Can't I be tired?

I was talking through my teeth and everyone around us was silent.

Let's just go home, he said, so we left with no groceries and he made us box pasta with jar sauce and we
didn't speak and I got into bed even though it was
barely eight and my husband sat beside the bed like
he was well and I was ill and I began to feel that
way—my illness became truer and truer, grew large,
filled the room, filled my body, filled my recent and
deeper past. When had I become so ill? Had I always
been this way?

Whatever it is, you can tell me, you know?

The wisp-thin crack in the ceiling reminded me of
bones and spines and the way they give up, eventually, and what happens to a body when it gives in to
time—Better not say anything about that, I thought; I
rolled to face the wall because I did not care for the
here or the now and I wondered whether we were
who we thought we were, if we were actually married
or just in a continuous situation with each other
and I wondered if my want to get up and leave him
was an indigenous want, something I had birthed, or
whether this want was foreign, a splinter, something
to pry out.

But I couldn't talk about any of that, so I rolled
back to him and said, *Tell me again.*

And he said, *Oh, is that what this is all about?*

And I said, *I don't know.*

It was true I had this need every autumn, reliable
as dried leaves.

She was wearing a light blue shirt, he said. *She was
holding a paper coffee cup. She put the cup down on my
desk, put her bag on the chair beside my desk, opened the*

*bag, and took out the papers. She handed them to me. She
asked me to check over them.*

Do you remember her shoes?

The red ones. The same red sneakers she always wore.

And her hair? Did she have it up?

*It was down and uncombed. It was in her face a little.
She looked tired. She looked out the window behind my
desk while she spoke. We didn't make eye contact. She told
me she would come get the papers tomorrow.*

But she must have known that she wouldn't come
get the papers tomorrow, unless she hadn't yet decided about tomorrow, and if she had really said she
was coming to get the papers tomorrow maybe that
meant the whole thing had been an accident, or did
it mean she had acted on some fleeting thought that
wasn't what she really believed, or did it mean nothing? I have never really stopped thinking of how the
smartest person I knew had, after much thought, decided that life was not worth it—that she'd be better
off not living—and how was I supposed to live after
that?

After some time my husband reached over to hold
my hand, which reminded me that at least there was
this, at least we still had hands that remembered
how to love each other, two bone-and-flesh flaps that
hadn't complicated their simple love by speaking or
thinking or being disappointed or having memories.
They just held and were held and that is all. Oh, to be
a hand.

Do you want to talk about her now?

And he knew I meant his mother, that it was his

turn to try to get near the loss that he couldn't get away from, those thoughts that came back each autumn just to die for him again, to remind him of what had happened, of how it felt.

Once she didn't pick me up at school and I walked home and when I got there it was dark and she hadn't made dinner but she said, You're late for dinner, *which I thought was funny because I was nine and didn't realize how sick she was. I told her I had walked home from school and she asked why my dad hadn't picked me up, and I said,* I don't have a dad, remember? *And she said,* Oh, that's right, *and I asked her why she was on the floor, and she told me she was tired, that she was too tired to get up.*

I knew what he'd say next, but I always listened intensely, as if I was trying to memorize his pain so I could re-create it once he was gone or dead or dead and gone, because I thought, at the time, that my husband's loss was what I had really fallen in love with, and maybe that loss was locked up in my husband like a prison and this was our once-a-year meeting and so I had to press myself against the Plexiglas to feel the blood and body heat of his loss, stare hard at the loss so I could remember how its face was shaped, the exact color of its eyes, something to get me through the next year of living with my husband and not his loss, but the lack of his loss, a bleached-out version of it, a numb heart that hosted something with a real pulse and wildness because my husband had only the most basic pulse and absolutely no wildness, but his loss was wild, was wild and filled with fast blood, and I could understand that angry bright red thing. I knew it was possible that I was not in love with a person but a person-shaped hole.

Kids can understand sometimes, he said. *She was missing something. I don't know what she was missing.*

Did you know that she would go the way she did?

When I was a kid I knew she was leaving, sort of slowly, but I didn't know what that meant. Just that there was less of her all the time. Every year more of her was gone.

I asked him questions like this even though it made my husband suffer, like a child pinching leaves off a fern frond.

Did you know it was going to happen to Ruby?

No, I said, *not really. Did you know?*

We barely knew each other, Elly. We hardly ever spoke.

And this is what he always said and what I always had a hard time believing, that he barely knew her, and I thought of Ruby and my husband in his office and how he'd look at her equations, not at her face, and I thought of them in his classroom when she was his TA and how she could have heard his chalk click on the board there, and now that same noise woke me up some nights and Ruby knew this noise before I did and what did that mean? What did it mean that she knew something that I would eventually know, that her dying made my life take this turn? I sometimes thought that my husband's pain had radiated out of him and into Ruby's blood and turned her against herself, that it was his fault somehow that Ruby pushed out the screen in the women's room and put herself into the air, but I also knew (though I maybe didn't know that I knew) that she had come to this conclusion on her own, though I still sometimes imagined my husband had sent a signal out the way bats or plants sometimes do. My husband knew what a woman looked like before she threw herself out of this world and he knew Ruby before she threw herself out of this world and I will never be able to divide those two things.

I wanted him to be responsible for how Ruby went missing, and I know that no one gets back what they lose this way and he wouldn't and I wouldn't, but at the same time I wanted it back and couldn't stop wanting it back and if I couldn't get it back I wanted, at least, for someone or something to be at fault—I wanted him to be responsible for how Ruby went missing.

I am or we were (or still are) the kind of people who can never quite get away from our losses, the kind of people who don't know that magic trick that other people seem to know—how to dissolve a sense of loss, how to unbraid it from a brain.

The morning after our box pasta dinner and loss thumbing, I went to the clinic to give them the blood and information I said I'd give them. It was for a study, and I didn't know exactly what they were looking for, only that I had agreed to do it as a favor to some colleagues of my husband's.

Reliable participants were hard to find, they said.

Reliable participants would do the following:

Arrive at seven in the morning each Tuesday on an empty stomach, bleed a tube of blood for a nurse, allow the lab technician with the large, soft hands to apply the electrodes, answer the questions he asked (*What do you believe in? What is your greatest fear? What is the point of love?*), bleed more blood, drink a blue liquid, sit in a dark room for fifteen minutes, answer questions in the dark (*Do you believe inner peace is possible? Is there an afterlife? What is something you know is true?*), give more blood, eat a complimentary pack of graham crackers and a carton of juice so you don't pass out on the subway or sidewalk, go home, and receive a check for ninety dollars each Friday.

As they took the blood, I watched the thin, clear tube turn red and I felt it get warm against my forearm and I thought about how my hands and my husband's hands still loved each other and how the rest of our bodies just dangled off these hands and I envied how simply those hands could be what they were—ambivalent chunks of bone and muscle that just touch, hold, and are held, repeat. And maybe, I thought, if I was lucky, this study could end up making my blood and brains feel better, less driven by dread, less stuck on what is missing. But part of the point of this study was that I not know the study's point, which made it seem a lot like everything.

10

Have you seen that? the old lady asked, tilting her head toward two large white buildings built to look like a sheep and a dog.

Oh, what are they?

A sheep and a dog, she said.

But what's inside?

Buildings, she said. *They made them to look like animals. It's funny.*

She pulled over in front of a café with a sign that said THE INTERNET. I got out of the car and the old lady said, *Good luck, take care*, and I didn't know what I was going to spend any good luck on or what I could care for, but I said, *Thank you*, because that's what you do.

A woman was sitting at an old, beige machine while a dial tone droned and hissed and beeped and fractured into static. She glanced at me and smiled. Ambiguously familiar pop music was playing, an excited woman singing like a maniac, an excited maniac, about something exciting, about how good it all was, how good it would always be. The woman hummed along to the music, seeming so content with the static still hissing, the nothing happening. The amount of patience in this country—how long a person could spend happily waiting—maybe this was why I had come here. Not for the isolation, but the place where people can happily do very little, the world's largest waiting room.

It took a moment for me to remember how to log into my email or what email even was, what any of those words on the screen meant. My boss's name appeared a few times, which didn't make any difference to me since I knew I didn't work there anymore. There were a few emails from Husband: apologies for whatever he had done, demands of apologies from me, apologies for the demands of apologies, demands—again—for some kind of sense to be made of everything, for me to pay him what I owed him, pay him in my time and life, to pay off the hurt I'd done by stealing myself—I was his, he said, I belonged to him, to us, to our future, and didn't I understand that? How did I not understand that? What had I done with that understanding?

The most recent was only a few minutes old:

I know you're not at your mother's, Elyria. I didn't want to, but I looked through your emails, hoping to figure something out and, well, I don't know what to say. Call me. Whatever time it is. I am barely ever sleeping now, so you won't wake me up . . .

And there was also a two-word note from Mother: *Everything okay?*

Those words just sat there—*everything okay?*—as if we understood each other so well that this kind of shorthand was even possible—*everything okay?*—and I knew that she knew that nothing was okay, that she wasn't and I wasn't and we had never been, and I remembered, too, this was also what she had asked, years ago, when I told her over lunch that I was going to marry the professor.

Oh, honey . . .

And she put a hand on my hand as if I was her honey—

Is everything okay?

The main thing that wasn't okay in that moment was her hand on my hand, so I took my hand back and I asked her what that was supposed to mean, and I was thinking of how terrible it is that everyone has to be a child of a person, and why would someone want to make more people when it all just leads up to sitting in an expensive midtown restaurant on an overcast Tuesday trying to eat a poached egg that's gone cold under hollandaise congealed like pale yellow blood, talking about whether anything is *okay*.

It just seems odd. I mean, Ruby's professor? Like, her boss? That skinny boy with the big jacket? I mean, sure, get yourself a first ex-husband, whatever, but I just don't think he's right for you.

And I knew that it was possible he wasn't entirely *right* for me, but I also knew, in some way, that probably no one was right for me and potentially no one was right for anyone, but I also felt, with uncharacteristic sincerity, that we were as right for each other as any two people could manage, and I had chosen life in the face of death, this was how the professor said it, that since his mother had died he had been choosing to *live* every day, and I took this to mean he was just trying to do the best he could do with his life, to pretend to be the better version of himself even if he couldn't always be that better version of himself, the version that can appropriately adjust to the disappointments of life, and let go of irrevocable losses, and stay awake through entire days without falling asleep in the middle of work or the middle of a subway car or the middle of a sentence.

Everything is okay, I told my mother back then, as someone was taking the plates away (*All done?*) and she said, again, *Oh, honey*, and I still wasn't her honey and I clenched my jaw and she said, *It's depression, honey, you're just depressed. You just need to have someone give you something. You don't need to get married, that's not going to fix anything, believe me, it won't.*

I'm not trying to fix anything.

Oh, honey.

Stop calling me honey.

He doesn't have anything to do with Ruby anymore and he's not going to bring her back.

I didn't ask to bring her back, I said, and this may or may not have been the moment I got up and put on my jacket and Mother said, *Oh, I just don't understand you and your moods, why you can't just control yourself*, or maybe she didn't say anything right then, maybe she just got out a compact to look at and powder her nose and I knew that's what she probably did after she wrote that one-line email, that *everything okay?* She probably looked into a mirror to make sure her nose was still sitting on her face as usual, and I'm not one of those people who think of the right thing to say at the right moment, so that day at the restaurant I didn't try to explain myself or my moods or my lack of an ability to control myself and that other day I didn't write her any reply to her one-line email, didn't tell her anything was okay or not okay.

I paid the woman for the minutes of Internet and she said, *Thank you so much*, and she seemed to mean it more than the average person.

There was a diner across the road and I went into it and took a whole booth for my little self. I stared at the menu and did not think of my husband. I stared at the tile floor and did not think of where I was or why I was here. A waitress came by and I told her what I wanted to eat, which seemed suddenly a very personal thing to tell a stranger, what things you were going to turn into your body. She asked me if I was traveling by myself and I said I was and she said, *Aw, good-onya, brave little one you are, don't get too lonely, do you?*, and I smiled so gently and did not throw the salt shaker across the restaurant.

After a while the old man at the booth beside mine leaned over—

Where are you from?

So I told him where I was from and he asked me where I was going and I said, *The South Island ferry*, and he said, *Today?* And I said, *Whenever*.

Well, he said, *I'm on my way back to Taupo if you'd like a ride. I make this drive fairly often and even though I'm old I'm still a good driver, so you shouldn't worry about that.*

Oh. Okay.

The reason I make this drive so much is that I put my wife in a home up here so she could be with her sister. She doesn't like it there, but she didn't like living with me either. She likes when I come visit, is what she says, but she isn't really sure who I am and she doesn't understand that I'm her husband. Isn't that too bad?

The man looked at me then went back to looking out the window. No one likes to be unrecognizable. No one wants to be a stranger to someone who is not a stranger to them.

There's not much for me anywhere, he said, but he didn't sound sad. *My orchard has dried up, my wife's brain is gone, my children moved to Australia. Even my only grandson died. Leukemia. That never made any sense to me and never will.*

He shook his head and smiled.

But this is a nice place. Good pies. Nice waitresses. It's a perfect place to stop on the way to Taupo. It's a very nice place. There are still a lot of nice places like this, you know, even though lots of other things have gone wrong. You're not in a hurry to get to the South Island, are you?

It seemed to take a reason to be in a hurry and I didn't have any reasons, I knew, and maybe *that* was it, maybe I had come to New Zealand to find a reason in this quiet country where everyone was happily waiting on almost nothing, to wait with them until a reason found me or I found a reason.

You should never be in a hurry if you can help it. It's bad for everything. Bad for the stomach, the spleen, the skin. Especially bad for the joints. The knees and ankles. Rushing isn't healthy at all.

Eventually the old man drove me to his house out-side Taupo and he told me that I could go waterskiing and hang gliding and kayaking because there was a lake nearby and people in that lake did things like that, but I didn't tell the old man that I didn't want to ski or glide or yak because that was not the kind of per-son that I was and I was not on an adventure and I was not a tourist and I was just a person. I smiled and said, *Oh, that sounds nice,* and he said, *It is, it's nice, it's a nice place. I've lived here for about thirty years and it's very nice.*

I woke at four the next morning in the old man's guest bedroom, which was actually not a guest bed-room but the abandoned room of his daughter: pink quilts, pink walls, gymnast trophies, and a dusty doll-house. I had slept in my clothes so I just got up and put my shoes on and left and walked far.

11

How funny (or not funny) that the old man (all alone in his four-bedroom farmhouse on the edge of a dried-up orchard with a garage full of small engine parts for the plane he'd never built) had a life that had gotten up and run away from him (his daughters in other countries and last names, his wife forgetting everything, his grandson in some other dimension, his apple trees diseased and fruitless, and his incomplete engines rust-thick) while I, instead, had been the thing running from my whole life.

The sky was brightening slowly as I walked into Taupo, past a parking lot full of boats, down a highway just east of the lake, and though I can sometimes think back and romanticize this moment, the sheer morning glow, the cloudless sunrise, I know that all I was really thinking about in that objectively beautiful moment was whether I'd even had a choice when it came to leaving my husband, and whether we are, like Ruby had once said we were, just making decisions based on inner systems we have little to no control in creating—and I thought of that professor who became my husband and I thought of the sensation that came after he put a hand on my shoulder, a sensation that had turned me more human, put me in contact with what I think I was supposed to be feeling, and how it allowed me to be destroyed by the leaving of Ruby because being occasionally destroyed is, I think, a necessary part of the human experience. Before he put his hand on my shoulder I suspected that somewhere in me or near me was the appropriate human reaction for that moment and after he put his hand on my shoulder the appropriate human reaction made itself evident, and when he touched my shoulder, he also seemed to have come into contact with the emotional reality that he needed to experience. We both cried and the fluorescent light tinted our skin blue and I could see right through his skin to a vein in his face, a tiny blue vein on his forehead made bluer in the blue light and we held hands—it somehow made sense to hold hands with this stranger in ways it had never made sense to hold the hand of any other stranger—and Mother came back in and sat beside me and put a hand on my shoulder and nothing happened, nothing changed, nothing felt better, because she didn't have the same effect on me that this professor had on me and I didn't know why that was then, but I am coming nearer to understanding it now. Some people make us feel more human and some people make us feel less human and this is a fact as much as gravity is a fact and maybe there are ways to prove it, but the proof of it matters less than the existence of it—how a stranger can show up and look at you and make you make more sense to yourself and the world, even if that

sense is extremely fragile and only comes around occasionally and is prone to wander or fade—what matters is that sometimes sense is made between two
people and I don't know if it's random or there is any
kind of order to it, what combinations of people work
the best and why and how do we find these people
and how do we keep these people around, and I don't
know if it's chaos or not chaos but it feels like chaos
to me so I suppose it is.

My mother looked at me, her only surviving and
previously not-prone-to-weeping daughter now all wet-
faced with this man in a poorly cut suit, and she put
her hand out to him and said, *Ruby's mother; I'm Ruby's
mother*, and he shook it, then Mother got up as if
that was the last thing she had to do and she left and
didn't tell me where she was going and I didn't care
where she was going because I was in a more human
state—I was making sense to myself—I was making
sense to this man and we were making sense to each
other. We went to a diner and tried to eat but couldn't,
so we mostly sat in silence and a woman came around
refilling our coffee to a constant brim and we just
held each other's hands and we seemed to know something that we had not previously known.

In that dark autumn and even darker winter we
kept meeting for coffee, meeting in parks and plazas
and diners and having long hugs and before this I had
not been the type of person to want to hug a person,
but now I didn't even think of who I had previously
been and what I had previously done because now the
only thing that made sense was our shaking chests

pressed together because when we were together we were alive and human in a way we had not found in other parts of life, and we would spend hours sitting on benches in cold parks until it got dark and we would go and eat something together and we did this many days in a row, then after a few months we went to his apartment while it was snowing and we fucked like our lives depended on it, like every life on the planet depended on it, like the concept of death depended on it, like the state of being a human, and being alive, in general, depended on our fucking. And this went on for a while and I became a haver-of-authentic-emotions, an openhearted, well-adjusted, and thriving person, a dependable employee, a woman who could go out to a deli and order a sandwich and eat it and read the newspaper like a grown woman without thinking of the sentence *I am being a grown woman, eating off a plate, and reading the news*, because I was not an observer of myself, but a be-er of myself, a person who just *was* instead of a person who was almost.

For a year or so I thought that was how it would always be, that I had achieved some plane of existence that was better than the one I'd been on previously and there was no going back, but I was wrong and there was going back and I went back, I went back and forth, and forth and back again—

I would sometimes think of my husband smiling and the thought of him smiling would make me smile but hours later I would think of my husband again and I wouldn't smile—I'd think, *Husband, what do you think you're smiling for, there's nothing to smile about*, and

I would think that wasn't the kind of thought that I wanted to have, but I *had* had it, and then I couldn't think of my husband smiling anymore because every time I thought of him he was frowning a pissed-off frown and later I would think, *Husband, please smile again*, and sometimes, after a while, the thought of my husband would smile again and I would think, *Oh, good, we're fine, we are human, we love each other like adults should, we are grown people*. And this went on for some time and sometimes it was easier to keep the thought of my husband smiling and sometimes it was harder to keep the thought of my husband smiling. As the years went on I sometimes could have sworn that the existence of my husband and the whole complicated mess of him in my life was everything that was wrong with being alive and if I only extracted myself from him everything might go back to making sense the way it had when we had been new to each other. If he was no longer a part of my life then the fact that he was no longer a part of my life would be *new* and maybe the newness was what had made me make sense to myself—not him, another human, just fallible and breakable and not capable of creating redemption— because that's the thing: people can't really redeem people and I don't know what redeems people, what keeps people good, what keeps people in the sense-making part of being a human instead of the senseless, the unwell, the wildebeests that everyone has—because we all have them and there is a part of every human brain that just can't bear and be, can't sit up straight, can't look you in the eye, can't sit through time tick-ing, can't eat a sandwich off a plate, can't read the newspaper, can't put on clothes and go somewhere, can't be married, can't keep looking at the same person every day and being looked at by the same person every day without wanting to make him swallow a tiny bomb and set that bomb off and make him disappear, go back in time and never get near this man who is looking at you and living with you and being so happy to just love and be loved and we all sometimes want to walk away like it never happened.

Isn't everyone on the planet or at least everyone on the planet called me stuck between the two impulses of wanting to walk away like it never happened and wanting to be a good person in love, loving, being loved, making sense, just fine? I want to be that person, part of a respectable people, but I also want nothing to do with being people, because to be people is to be breakable, to know that your breaking is coming, any day now and maybe not even any day but this day, this moment, right now a plane could fall out of the sky and crush you or the building you're in could just crumble and kill you or kill the someone you love—and to love someone is to know that one day you'll have to watch them break unless you do first and to love someone means you will certainly lose that love to something slow like boredom or festering hate or something fast like a car wreck or a freak accident or flesh-eating bacteria—and who knows where it came from, that flesh-eating bacteria, he was such a nice-looking fellow, it is such a shame—and your wildebeest, everyone's wildebeest, just wants to get it over with, can't bear the tension of walking around the world as if we're always going to be walking around the world, because we're not, because here comes a cancer, an illness, a voice in your head that wants to jump out a window, a person with a gun, a freak accident, a wild wad of flesh-eating bacteria that will start with your face.

But my husband before he was Husband, being around him did, for a while, make me forget about my wildebeest. We walked around the city holding hands and we did a good deal of reflexive smiling and we often kissed and it felt like drugs that are too strong to legally exist outside of a body and there was that night the professor who became my husband smiled at me in the dark and I could see the pale white glow of his teeth and I thought there would never be anything better than seeing the pale white glow of his teeth through the dark on this night after we decided to get married and for at least a few minutes it made perfect sense and I believed that he had redeemed me and in a way he had and he did—but I don't know why the wildebeests kept coming back, throwing all their angry weight around and making all those sweet, human, cracked-open, genuine, well-adjusted feelings go away, but they did go away—why did they go away?—I would like them not to go away and I would like to go back to being or feeling redeemed by him, by the white glow of his teeth in the dark, by our skin against each other—*What are you thinking?* he asked me that night with his teeth, and I thought about what I was thinking about and I worried that I was slipping away from making sense, but I gripped hard on that sense and said, *Oh, nothing, just how I love you,* and I twisted my toes under the sheets and told myself to be a woman who lives normally, being loved and loving—and I could be her—couldn't I? Couldn't I?

12

After Taupo and some cars, I got to Wellington and I got all the way to the ferry station and I stared at it. I remembered what someone said once about traveling, that sometimes the body moves somewhere too quickly for the soul and the soul is taking its sweet-ass time to catch up because the soul is not on speaking terms with the body but regardless, the body is a lonely animal without the soul, so I thought, maybe it is time for me to sit very still and wait for the soul and I understood how melodramatic that was but I decided not to care because, after all, someone else had said it first and even though I couldn't remember exactly who it seemed that they were very old or European or both—someone somehow trustworthy.

I walked to a hostel and tried to pay for a room with a card and the girl behind the counter seemed embarrassed when it wouldn't go through a third time—*Oh, it's probably my fault*—so I paid for a night with one of the traveler's checks I'd brought to give me a false sense of having my shit together. I only had a few hundred dollars in checks because a false sense of having my shit together only cost a few hundred dollars. I left my backpack in my room and walked into the city, beside a museum, past a bank, past a library with wide windows. Businesspeople strolled around, looking for business.

I stepped into a nearly empty pub where the bartender was wiping the counter, leaning into his flexed arms, a swirl of black hair on his head like a cartoon of a mechanic in some imagined past. He seemed to immensely enjoy being himself, fashionably morbid, nostalgic for an era in which he was still dead. At the end of the bar was a woman who was maybe my age or younger. From the waist up she was waifish and pale, but her legs were gigantic, muscular logs— proportionally absurd, and I imagined taking her to a park where she could lie on the ground and I could nap on her legs, thick as mattresses as they were. It is a strange thing to want, the sexless bodily comfort of a stranger, but her legs seemed to be as long as a door and one was bent to her chest and the other dangled below like all this leg was just too much for her and there was something comforting about that surplus and I was low on comfort, on anything comfortable. A man with a bloated neck stared down the girl the way a dog stares down a steak.

Up close the bartender's face was boyish and pained, so much so I felt like his mother when I looked at him, and it was unbearable to see him so unhappy after all that I had gone through to bring him into the world. This was not a convenient feeling to have when all I wanted was to order a sandwich and beer. I took a stool facing away from the girl and pushed my bizarre feelings away for long enough to order and I got out a book to avoid looking at the bartender and as I read I half dreamed that the bartender asked me to read aloud to him, and so in my half dream, I did. At first he laughed at the right parts, he saw the quiet tragedy of *Mrs. Bridge* and I began to think that he had just the right measure of unhappiness and dissatisfaction with life to be someone I could get along with. In my half dream the bartender smiled and we made occasional, comfortable eye contact as I read, but then my fantasy turned sour, and he stopped laughing at any of the funny parts, stopped reacting entirely. He looked around for someone to pour a beer for and seemed dismayed when there was no one. He exhaled visibly. He cracked his knuckles.

Oh, this chapter's not as good out loud, I said in my half dream. *I'll read a different one.*

I flipped to the scene where Mrs. Bridge is trying to learn Spanish from a record, but I mangled the pronunciation and he had to correct me.

It's Cómo está usted.

Cómo está usted?

No. Cómo está usted.

I am a stupid American, I thought inside the fantasy inside my thought as I read *Mrs. Bridge*, as the imagined bartender wiped a white towel down the bar, inching away. I decided in my fantasy I would make an effort to speak in a way that was more pleasing to listen to and I would choose a passage better suited for the bartender: the part where Mrs. Bridge, sleepless, has a growing sense of unreality and despair.

She had a feeling that all was not well and she waited in deep expectancy for some further intimation, listening intently, but all she heard before falling asleep was the familiar chiming of the clock.

(The imagined bartender began wiping down the bar again, moving toward me.)

The next morning Lois Montgomery telephoned to say that Grace Barron had committed suicide.

(And he was visibly satisfied with the sudden darkness, and I knew that I'd found a way to capture his attention, though I wasn't sure what use I had for his attention.)

In the days that followed Mrs. Bridge attempted to suppress this fact. Her reasoning was that nothing could be gained by discussing it; consequently she wrote to Ruth that there was some doubt as to what had been the cause of Mrs. Barron's death but it was presumed she had accidentally eaten some tuna-fish salad which had been left out of the refrigerator overnight and had become contaminated, and this was what she told Douglas and Carolyn.

(The imagined bartender kept listening and I thought, as I read, inside my thought, that maybe in another dimension this bartender *was* my child and this was our alternate-universe bedtime story, in the middle of the day, in the middle of a bar, in the middle of my head.)

Her first thought had been of an afternoon on the Plaza when she and Grace Barron had been looking for some way to occupy themselves, and Grace had said, a little sadly, "Have you ever felt like those people in the Grimm fairy tale—the ones who were all hollowed out in the back?"

The idea of my alternate-universe bedtime story dissolved and I left money on the bar and I got up, denied myself a glance at the woman who owned those legs, and wandered away, first to the library where an email from my husband let me know he'd canceled all my credit cards and closed my bank account and that explained it, so I went back to the hostel and counted the money I had: two hundred American dollars in traveler's checks, twenty-seven New Zealand dollars, thirty-eight New Zealand cents, and one American nickel. I thought about this, remembering that when he took over all our finances after the wedding I somehow hadn't considered any of the ways that it might become a problem, then lay on the bunk and saw that on the underside of the mattress above mine someone had written THIS PLACE SUCKS.

13

In the morning I checked out of the hostel and walked slowly down the street. Three Japanese girls were posing in front of a mailbox; one pretended to kiss it while a fourth took a picture with her phone. I walked into a bookstore, half-intending to buy a book so I didn't have to read *Mrs. Bridge* again, but I noticed a flyer by the door:

What Do You Need? A Home? A Job? Advice?

In smaller letters it asked:

Do You Need To Know Something? Do You Need To Know Someone? Are You Wandering? What If You Had A Place To Stay? Are You Out Here Reading A Flyer And Saying Yes, That Is Me? Some People Are In Need Of Giving; Do You Know Any People Like That? Would You Like To?

There was a name, Dillon, and a number. I wondered for a while why he had capitalized every word on his flyer, then I memorized the number, left the bookstore, found a phone booth, and called.

This is Dillon; may I help? he said after one ring.

I saw your flyer.

And what would you like to tell me?

I'm traveling and need to make some money.

Did you know that no one ever calls from that flyer?

No, I didn't know that.

Has it ever occurred to you that no one wants to ask for help?

Well, I said, wondering if that was what I was doing—asking for help. That was supposedly the first step in something, in making progress, in becoming a better person with fewer problems. Or wait—was it admitting you have a problem? But doesn't everyone have problems? Isn't waking up or drinking water or eating lunch admitting you have a problem? There was a long silence going on. I realized I had stopped talking in the center of a sentence.

Do you have a pen? Can you take down this address?

I was happy he let me stay in my other world where sentences didn't have endings.

The neighborhood I walked through on the way to Dillon's seemed like nice families lived inside all the houses, like there was always a woman cooking something inside them all and these nice houses reminded me of a story I'd heard about a woman who'd had enough of her children: One morning after her husband had driven off she dressed the children, a small boy and two very small twin girls, and she put them in the minivan and she drove the minivan to a police station and she took the children out of the minivan and she told them to hold each other's hands and not to speak, that whatever happened, they should just say nothing, and she led the children into the police station and she told an old man at the front desk, *These children—I found these children. I do not know who they belong to or where they should go*, and she turned and walked out and got into her minivan and drove home and took a nap and that evening when her husband came home and said, *Dear, where are the children?*, she said, *What children?* The husband said he could see in her eyes that she had gotten up and left herself and isn't that the worst kind of leaving? No one is okay when someone leaves like that and I knew I never wanted to leave that way. I can't quite remember the end of the story but I thought it somehow involved the husband going to the police station to retrieve his children and finding that they hadn't said a word all day.

Dillon's house was slumping into itself on the edge of a hill.

Welcome! someone shouted as I stood in the street and stared.

I couldn't see who had shouted. I looked to see if maybe they were behind me.

Over here! the same voice said.

I looked at what I thought was over there, then I looked at another there, but I didn't see anyone.

Hello?

Come on up, someone said, and I couldn't quite tell if it was the same voice or a different one. A tree rustled and a man jumped out of it, in a kind-of-like-falling way, and he landed on a wooden balcony on the second floor of the house. He opened the door to the balcony and went in, then came out the other side, the door at the top of the stairs I was climbing.

Are you my flyer reader? he asked.

Yes, I said, regretting it with every part of myself. He had three or four dreadlocks tailing the back of his head but the rest of his hair was cut short, shoe-polish black. A silver ring hung on one nostril and his body was put together in a way that suggested it would be easy for him to move a large piece of furniture by himself.

Are you our traveler in need?

I guess?

You guess! Ha! You're great. You're a great one. All right, up you come—make haste, young rabbit! Make haste!

Looking back I realize I should have pretended to be at the wrong house, to be the wrong traveler, but for some reason, I made haste. In the living room a girl in a hemp dress and an Indian boy were talking about the sadness of a certain class of arachnids, the ones that carry poisons they don't have the ability to use. The boy was short and narrow, seemed barely fifteen. He wore a long, tan tunic trimmed with yellow embroidery. He was nodding his head and smiling and speaking lowly, intently, as if he was an incarnation of some god or saint. There were others there—Sia, the Italian girl who spoke in a voice so tiny it seemed whispered from her belly button, and Gian, who never said a word, and Marco, who said too many, and the British woman, who always kept her backpack locked shut in the corner, even while she showered or made dinner or spoke to someone about how safe she felt in New Zealand, not like the other places she had been and all the awful things that had happened.

That night I looked at the only picture I had of my husband. In it he is a baby in his mother's arms, a crumpled, fatty lump of who he eventually became, his little mouth hanging open, his mother looking distraught, caught between a hard place and another hard place—the rest of the family stands behind them, repetitive noses, eyes, skins, hairs, like wallpaper. And as I looked at the baby version of my husband, I decided not to call the present version of my husband anymore. I had called earlier that day from a pay phone near Dillon's house, but when he picked up it was only to thank me for calling and to ask me to not call again.

I said it was tomorrow where I was and he said, yes, he knew it was tomorrow there.

I have to go, he said, *but maybe you should call again. We should talk again. We should be trying to fix this, whatever this is. I feel strange that I haven't heard from you, but I feel strange talking to you, too. Actually, don't call anymore. I don't think it's a good idea.*

Okay, I said.

It will be better this way, if we just don't speak until you can tell me you're coming home.

The calmness in his voice wasn't at all convincing, and after I hung up the phone I imagined my husband told me he'd convinced the people in charge of the study to give him the information they'd gotten from me—the pictures of my brain, my answers, my data—and I imagined my husband saying this as if he was announcing a job promotion or that he had unexpectedly won a portion of a class-action lawsuit and as I walked back to Dillon's house I wondered if maybe I hadn't imagined my husband telling me this but maybe he'd really *said* it, really done it, and even though I understood why my husband might go to such anxious lengths to find out what, specifically, was wrong with me, this wasn't a nice thing to hear or imagine hearing, and the little throbbing anger under everything my husband had said reminded me of how unfair feelings could be, of how our feelings had hunched up and backed away from us, left us looking at each other like strangers.

Hours later, falling asleep on a floor, I couldn't quite parse a difference between what I'd imagined him saying and what he had actually said and I looked at the photograph of my husband again, the baby him, the he that he was long before we met, before I had even been born, and I remembered that morning when he told me I had lost my mind.

Okay, I said. *You're probably right. Do you want tea?*

The things I disagreed with the most adamantly were often the most true, so I wanted to see what would happen if I just agreed. Maybe if I agreed he would have to be wrong and maybe this was the trick of being married to my husband: agreement.

I thought, for one nice moment, that I had discovered something, and then my husband asked if I was aware that I'd lost my mind or if it was something I was managing to overlook. I couldn't tell if he was kidding or not. He was never much of a kidder.

You know, I think I'll make some coffee instead of tea, I said. *Would you like some?*

It's a problem I've always had— doing the domestic things I didn't actually want to do, but it always seemed to me that if I didn't do them then they would never get done.

I'm asking you a question, he said. *And it's an important question. And it's important to me that you think about it, that you think about what I'm asking you.*

Okay, I said. *You're right.*

Agreement.

I knew how he took his coffee, black and luke-warm, so I poured him a cup and I dropped an ice cube in.

On Dillon's floor I tried to fall asleep by thinking of ice cubes melting in hot coffee and I thought of wild animals chewing smaller wild animals and I remembered what that nurse had said about the tubes of blood, that they always went to a safe place, and I wondered if my husband could have actually, in real life, talked to the neuroscientists from the study and I knew I didn't want my husband to know all the facts about my blood and brain because that would give him another unfair advantage. I told myself that the neuroscientists had not, of course, told him anything, that they were trustworthy, that they kept their sides of agreements, and I remembered the tall, black-haired lab technician with the large, soft hands who had spread the cold jelly over my scalp and slid all the electrodes in between my hair, gently, like I was his child, and I believed he would never do anything wrong to me, the cold jelly on his fingers, a warm hand on my shoulder. As I fell asleep that night on a floor it didn't matter what I feared or imagined my husband knowing or saying he knew because there was so much in me that he could never know and he would never know enough about me, and I wasn't really certain of that, but *See if I care*, I whispered, to nobody, to my husband, to my own self, see if my self cares, self, see if it cares.

14

Jaye was as temporary as me—a favor to Bill, the owner of the catering company who pinched her ass and called her the hottest transsexual flight attendant in Wellington, which raised the question of how many transsexual flight attendants were presently in Wellington. After a few weeks of these catering gigs that Dillon had helped me get, Jaye was the only person I had talked to for longer than the cursory where-are-you-from-where-are-you-going conversation. Outsiders recognize outsiders, I guess, though most of what she talked to me about was how being trans doesn't make you an outsider in Wellington because everyone here is so welcoming and tolerant and fabulous, how *no* one talks shit to *any*one and even if someone *did* try to start shit, someone else would fuck that person up for even trying to start shit or talk shit in the first place. This is just what Jaye told me. I didn't hear anyone talk shit about anyone or see anyone else fuck someone up for talking or starting shit in the first place.

A lady in a floor-length gown pointed at my platter—*What is it?*

I have no clue, I said, smiling like a Cheshire cat who had been drinking a stolen bottle of champagne in a broom closet.

You're cheeky, she said with a little curl in her voice.

Someone else asked, *Is this vegetarian? Is it gluten? I don't do gluten.*

It's all poison, I said. *The host is trying to poison you.*

I'd expected someone to report all my sassing, but they didn't. Sequined dresses laughed, cuff links slipped me business cards, and by the end I was invited to their afterparties because there is a certain kind of person who, when insulted, will assume you have something they need.

There will be many powerful men there, most of them at least partially eligible, a woman with too many teeth said as she scrawled an address on a soggy napkin. *Understand?* An ice sculpture of a sumo wrestler melted behind her; a dozen damp prawns bowed to it.

A couple times each hour Jaye would pull me into the broom closet and we'd drink straight from our stolen bottle and eat the hors d'oeuvres too ugly to pass. Jaye told me all the gossip she'd overheard at the party, how someone's third wife had come in the same dress as the first ex-wife and the ex-wife's second husband was having an affair with the sister of the ex-wife's first husband and it reminded me of the soaps, the useless drama of it, how it was just the same story of who someone had fucked or wanted to no longer fuck or wanted to fuck over or had already fucked over.

Jaye said she knew I had secrets—

I can smell a good secret, sugarpie, nothing gets past me. You're running from something and it was just a matter of what. Spill it—was it a lover? Money troubles? Caught your man with some slut?

I don't know, I said, I had to leave, so I did. That's all.

Jaye said, *Sluts don't judge, honey. A true slut don't ever, ever judge.* She pursed her lips for a second and said nothing because she was the truest kind of true slut. Her hands were cradling my face like a blossom.

He doesn't know where you are, does he?

I took a slug of the champagne then tried and failed to smile.

I see people like you all the time in the air. You see them drinking too much of the little wine bottles, asking for doubles of tequila on a midday flight. There's a spill on row seven, the girls say. Somebody's spilled all over the place, you get me?

Jaye laughed and apologized for laughing.

I left a note saying I went to my mother's house. I didn't say why.

Here's a stupid question: Why don't you just leave the mate? I mean really leave him, not just the country he's in.

Something is wrong with me, I said, smiling slack and champagne drunk.

What I meant was I knew I had to do something that I didn't know how to do, which was leaving the adult way, the grown-up way, stating the problem, filling out the paperwork, doing all those adult things, but I knew that wasn't the whole problem, that I didn't just want a divorce from my husband, but a divorce from everything, to divorce my own history; I was being pushed by currents, by unseen things, memories and imaginations and fears swirled together—this was one of those things you figure out years later but it's not the kind of thing you can explain to an almost-stranger in a broom closet while you're mostly drunk and you barely know where you are or why you are there or why some people can smell secrets.

Nothing is wrong with you, sugar, Jaye said, and I knew she thought that was true, but she didn't know about that wildebeest that lived in me and told me to leave that perfectly nice apartment and absolutely suitable job and routines and husband who didn't do anything completely awful—and I felt that the wildebeest was right and I didn't know why and even though a wildebeest isn't the kind of animal that will attack, it can throw all its beastly pounds and heavy bones at anything that attacks it or stands in its way, so I took that also into account. One should never provoke or disobey a wildebeest, so I did leave, and it seems the wildebeest was what was wrong with me, but I wasn't entirely sure of what was wrong with the wildebeest.

15

Jaye told me where to be and when to be there, so I did what she said. I got there early and waited for twenty minutes, then she splashed into the park: gold heels, a tangle of necklaces, bangles, earrings, a purple minidress struggling over her thighs.

Hello, my sunshine-doll-face-love!

Hi, Jaye.

So, last day in Welly, my little world traveler. I hope you won't forget the little people here in Wellywood.

She peck-kissed both sides of my face.

I smiled dumbly at her and she kept talking, telling me everything we had to do and see in the few hours before my ferry left. We walked into a bakery with tiny white tiles on the floor and a ceiling fan that was barely moving.

This place is run by a bunch of queers and queens and they make the best apricot slice in the whole fucking goddamn world. Can't even smell one without gaining a thousand bloody kilos.

She ordered an apricot slice and a drag queen handed it to Jaye wrapped in hot-pink wax paper. She took huge bites as we walked down the sidewalk, crumbs caked to her makeup.

I decided then that I was in love with Jaye—not a romantic love or a friendship one or a sexual one— it's some other kind that is clean and plain and harmless. It is a love made of an inaudible noise, like the noise that comes out of those whistles that only dogs can hear, or those little plastic things that people put on their cars so deer will hear them and get off the highway. But there is nothing to be done about the inaudible noise. It's just something that is.

And you're going where next?

Golden Bay. To that poet's farm.

Oh for fuck's sake.

What?

It's just—you know, there's nothing better about living in a farm than living in a city. Tourists are always coming here shitting themselves over nature—oh, it's so beautiful oh, there's no pollution, oh, goblins and hobbits and some such—but it's not a bloody magic show! It's not a movie. What's going to happen out there is you'll see a fuckload of possums and you'll be bored off your rocker. You can't just go sit in a pretty landscape and bet on it changing you into a better person.

I know, I said, because I had lost track of the hope I'd ever had to become a better person. *I know it's not a movie. I just want to be alone.*

I just don't see what's wrong with Wellington—you could stay here and do catering gigs, maybe meet a bloke or two—that'll get your mind off hubby, won't it?

The plan has been to go to Werner's. That's the plan.

Then what?

I don't know. I'll just be there.

For Christmas?

I shrugged. It was hard for me to imagine Christmas happening in the summer after almost three decades of Christmas in the cold. Maybe Christmas didn't exist this year.

You should come up to Napier and see me and the fam. Mum has a humongous place up there and it's always packed with weirdos and orphans for the holidays. You'll fit right in, love, a proper holiday with a proper dysfunctional family.

I hugged Jaye, falling into her hulking body. She patted my head.

Oh, honey, you are such a mess.

I'm fine, I said. *I'll be fine.*

Sure you will.

Jaye held my hand and I heard the inaudible noise and it turned into a color and that shade soaked into everything and my whole life was much nicer for those few minutes, then the sidewalk ended and we reached a huge hill with a hole cut through the center that cars were driving through.

You know I hate dirt, but I wanted to show you this trail so you know we have a little bit of nature here in Wellington, she said, pointing to a trailhead. *You go ahead and have a wee tramp if you like—I'll take the bus to meet you up top.*

When she told me she thought I'd want a little hike, I realized that a few minutes alone was exactly what I needed, something to make it possible for me to deal with the potency of the inaudible noise and of course Jaye would know that because all my real feelings and wants traveled in the inaudible noise, this current between us, so she could know things about me before I even knew things about me—this was what the inaudible noise could do. The trail was dark and had a thick, wooden smell in it. The trees were mythically large and sometimes looked more like art than life. Halfway up the hill I saw a man with a sack-belly hanging over red basketball shorts. He was leaning against a boulder, his face buried in the crook of his elbow as he was breathing heavily, like something terrible was happening inside his body.

Are you okay?

He gasped and stood up straight.

I'm fine, he said, but he didn't sound fine.

I heard something moving in the leaves.

I can get you help— Do you have a phone? I can go call someone for you. I have a friend at the top and—

I'm fine, he said, but sweat was rushing off his face. *You can just leave me alone. I'm fine.*

It was only then I noticed a younger man crouched on the ground beside the boulder. There was dirt on his face and he was sweating, too. His mouth made some kind of smile and his eyes spun as if he was a toy designed to look that way. I kept hiking up.

My love-face-darlin'-sweet-pea! Jaye arched her back around the bench at the bus stop. *So did you have a lovely time with the nature? Did you eat bugs and see the birds fucking the bees and all that fabulous shit?*

I decided not to tell Jaye about the men. We stared down at the white houses and the blue ocean licking the rocky coast.

After Jaye walked me to the ferry station she in-sisted, again, that I come up to Napier because she had gotten Christmas and New Year's off this time—

You have to suck a lot of dick for that, I can tell you, but there's no shame in it, she said. *I get what I want. They get what they want. Who can tell who is getting used?*

She laughed that thick, syrupy laugh that seemed to rise up from her toes, like every cell of her body was making a tiny, deep laugh and they were all adding up.

So, I'll see you for Christmas? New Year's?

I'll try.

You won't try; you'll be there, she said, and I was mostly certain that she was wrong.

Over the loudspeaker the ferry captain said, *Good after-noon, all! Welcome to Tuesday afternoon! Tuesday! All day it'll be Tuesday, all afternoon, make no mistake!* I felt like Tuesday afternoon was his home and we were his most anticipated guests and that was a nice feeling, the feeling of being in someone's home just by being alive on a Tuesday.

There was a bar on the ferry because whenever people are testing gravity (in planes or ships or from great heights) something has to happen to diffuse the tension of being a human and breakable, of knowing no one gets to see all the spaces and times they would like to see in this life. Everyone at the bar had the same bitter, dumb look in their eye. The ocean rocked us.

I took the last stool, beside a man who was finish-ing a beer. He put down his glass, wiped his mouth, looked over his sleeve at me, and nodded a nothing nod, which was good because I didn't want to deal with a something nod. I wanted to deal with the ocean because the ocean was making the ferry sway, making liquid slosh out of all the pints held in nervy hands. I put my hand on the bar and into a puddle of something, wiped it on my leg, then put my needing eyes on the bartender and she came over, a porcelain-faced woman, a tender tender. She poured beers so gracefully that it seemed like a dance and she brought the beers to the nothing-nod man and me without any questions or mentions of money because that is what a tender thing she was.

I will go on loving her for the rest of my life.

I went outside after my beer and looked down into the ocean and saw a stingray flapping in the water, a jagged C torn into his body and ribbons of blood running out, same color as mine, as anything's, and I knew that stingray had been chewed by something because that is all the ocean is—a big hole full of things chewing each other—and it's odd that people go to the beach and stare at the waving water and feel relaxed because what they are looking at is just the blue curtain over a wild violence, lives eating lives, the unstoppable chew, and I wondered if any of those vacationing people feel all the blood rushing under the surface, and I wondered if the fleshy, dying underside of the ocean is what they're really after as they stare—that ferocious pulse under all things placid.

16

I got into the car even though it was exactly the kind of car they say to avoid. Doors all dented. A long-haired, bearded driver with a cigarette pinched in his thin lips. This looked like the beginning of a porno or slasher movie and I didn't want to be slashed or porned, but I did need to get about a hundred miles west of this parking lot and the sun was nearly setting and this car was the only one making an offer and I have always been unable to decline anyone's offer of almost anything.

Where you edded?

He was shirtless and had a body that suggested he lived on a cliff and the only way to get home was to climb it.

Takaka?

I was never sure how to pronounce it, which *ka* got the emphasis.

'Swearum edded. Get in.

He moved boxes of beer from the passenger seat to the back, which was piled with duffel bags of I don't know what. He wore sunglasses, a big, utilitarian pair that wasn't designed in this decade or even the decade before this one. I ducked into the passenger seat and hugged my backpack like an airplane flotation device. Reggae music loud, windows down, cigarette smoke ribboning around the car, then shooting out the window like it was late for something.

After a few minutes the man started to shout over the music in my general direction. He was saying things in varying tones, maybe telling me a story about the bridge we were driving over or the fields we were driving toward. His voice sounded like vinyl played backward. I understood nothing. I said, *Yeah, yeah,* and nodded my head and raised my eyebrows when he raised his eyebrows and said, *Oh.* Sometimes he would laugh and turn his head to see if I was laughing and of course I laughed. I laughed and laughed and laughed, then I stopped laughing.

He turned the music up, lit another cigarette, and opened a beer as we drove up a mountain, making hairpin turns at unadvisable speeds. My organs let me know how much they disapproved of where I was sitting—I couldn't remember why I had ever wanted to go anywhere at all.

We reached the top and the view was not spectacular. A curve of unremarkable green under a faint grey fog. He turned down the music and pulled the car over.

At's Ozzie, terr, see?

He pointed at a man sitting under a tree and eating something out of his hands. A motorbike leaned against the trunk.

Say yer my wife, you keen?

Sorry?

At's my mate Ozzie there and I'm keen to take the piss out of him. Ya keen? Haven't got to do much—maybe lemme put my arm round you or something.

All right, I said, hoping I hadn't agreed to anything disagreeable.

He got out of the car and I got out of the car and we walked over to Ozzie. Ozzie and the man talked fast in grumbles and smacked each other's back. Ozzie called him Judas.

Who's 'at here?

'Atsma wife, Annie, here.

Judas put his arm around me. I smiled and thought of the words *unreality* and *despair.*

Aye, Judas, ya crazy fucker, Ozzie said. *Aye, ya fucker, ya crazy fucker. D'you go out on the piss and wake up hitched, then? Ya crazy fucker!*

I shrugged.

A stubby for the missus? How'd the little wifey like a beer, eh?

Oh, that's okay, I said, but Ozzie was already handing me a squat, amber bottle and pulling two more out of a small cooler attached to his motorbike.

Let me, Judas said, popping my bottle's cap with a lighter.

Judas and Ozzie made more noises that seemed to be words about some piece of machinery that Ozzie owned, something that Judas apparently had repaired or broken—their sentences half grumble and all slang. I looked down the neck of my beer and noticed that a dead bee was floating in it but kept drinking. Up the road at an abandoned-looking petrol station a man was dancing in the doorway to staticky music. The dancing man wore overalls and a little hat and moved his arms close to his body like he was running, but he wasn't going anywhere. A woman was laughing somewhere, but I couldn't tell if she was being entertained or tortured. A yellow pay-phone box was there, too, so I considered what would happen if I went over there and picked up the phone and called my husband, my actual husband, who, I knew, had supposedly lost any interest in where I was or where I was going or who I was getting married to out here in tomorrow, and just then my fake husband put a thick arm around me and as he pulled me closer, his fingers caught on a flimsy string of beads I was wearing, something one of Dillon's hippies had strung on me with no uncertain ceremony, and all the beads went scattering into the dirt. Ozzie howled.

Wee cracker of a lad you picked up here, wifey!

Ozzie went down to pinch up the little white and blue beads. Judas stared at me for a moment longer than I thought made sense.

Fuckin' hell, Annie. Sorry. Then he went to his knees, racing to collect them as if I was keeping time.

I took this moment to go to the pay phone and I called my husband despite all the reasons I had not to do that—I thought hearing him hear my voice would help me become a more accurate version of myself, that I might be able to understand who I was being if my husband could hear what I sounded like right then and reflect it back at me, and I thought I was ready to hear him and I thought he might have been ready to hear me, and I called for other reasons, too. An idle moment. A faked marriage with a stranger. The grey swamp between the day I left and where I was now. But instead of my husband, I just got some stale filler.

The number you have just dialed—

Not even a recorded version of his.

—is not available.

Just those machined words.

Please leave a message—

That metal woman.

Leave.

Please.

17

The second thing they tell you about hitchhiking is never accept invitations home for tea because tea really means dinner and dinner really means sex and sex really means they're going to kill you.

What's for tea, wifey? Ozzie asked as I came back from the pay phone.

Aye, there, she's my wifey, not yours! I've got a freezer to the lid with snappers if you're keen.

I'm keen, I said, thinking, What else could I be?

While he was frying the snappers, a splash of oil burned Ozzie's arm, but he just laughed a fat, heavy one and said, *Good as gold, goodasgold, goodasgold.* He showed me a few scars on his arms and a long, brutal one running down the side of his knee. *This one'll be a beaut,* he said, admiring the blister island filling with juice from somewhere deep inside him.

Judas had an old couch on his porch where we ate sitting in a row, but at first the plates were too hot to set on our bare knees, so we had to hold them by the edges, and the fish was too hot to eat so we just stared, a strange meditation, like this was our offering—slain, fried fish for some kind of god. After we ate, Ozzie and Judas went behind the house to deal with the machine they had been talking about earlier.

Be a good wifey, Judas said, kissing the top of my head. *We'll be out in the back with the beast.* Judas was still wearing his sunglasses and I realized I still hadn't seen my temporary husband's eyes.

Ozzie laughed. *Aye, the beast!* He punched Judas's arm.

I sat on the couch mostly asleep with my eyes open, thinking of nighttime ocean, listening to the black mumble of it out there. For a while I heard metal hitting metal, slowly at first then faster and faster, then a kind of sawing noise, then it all went away. Everything got quiet and I couldn't even hear Ozzie or Judas speaking. I wondered where they'd gone, what their mouths were doing if not filled with beer or barking at each other. The ocean kept mumbling.

The next morning I woke on that ratty sofa and went to find Judas and Ozzie asleep in the house on couches in front of a muted television. There was a close-up of a man in drenched white clothes, standing on a field, shaking fists above his head of bared teeth.

I'm leaving, I said.

Ozzie snored.

I'm leaving now, Judas . . . This is your wife. And I'm leaving.

I put my hands on my hips and spoke in Annie's voice.

I am leaving because I want a divorce. In fact, we're already divorced because I called a midnight lawyer and signed your name.

Judas didn't move. His mouth gaped like a slit in a fish belly and I saw his lip suck slightly in, then out again.

It's over! Over, over, over! Please do not attempt to contact me.

I went back out to the porch, swung my backpack on, walked out the side door and up the dirt path to the road. I was angry. I didn't know why I was angry but I knew that I was angry and I hadn't felt anger in so long it hit me harder, like coffee after weeks without, and this was the morning I wondered if all this aloneness was starting to sour me somehow, if I was becoming an increasingly ridiculous person— ridiculous for faking a twelve-hour marriage, faking a one-minute divorce, for leaving my real home and real husband, ridiculous for even thinking that leaving was ridiculous, because this was the decision that I had made because I am a person and people make decisions—yeses and noes—it's supposed to be like that.

A postman's truck had come up the road and stopped a few meters from me, so I walked over and got in. The postman had his hand on the door handle. He was frowning.

Where am I?

I hadn't meant to say that aloud. It was just what I was thinking.

Just east of Takaka. At the foot of Marble Mountain, the postman said. He let his hand drop off the handle and stopped frowning, as if he was happy to be reminded of where he was.

I didn't think Marble Mountain existed.

I suppose it doesn't. That's just what people call it. It's not even a mountain. Just a big hill.

Isn't it also a song? Or a made-up place?

Could be.

I put my hands in my lap.

Listen, he said, *I wasn't actually stopping to pick you up. I have to make a drop here, make a delivery.*

No cars had driven by and I thought it might have been too early to get a ride from anyone but him, and while I was sitting there thinking this the postman got out, moved something out of the back of the truck, and I stopped thinking and instead watched a bird in a tree. She was moving her head up and down as if agreeing with the morning.

The postman got back into the truck and said he'd take me to town, so he did and when he let me out in a parking lot on a street that seemed to be the entirety of Takaka, I stood still for a moment and smiled at the postman while I thought of that bloody stingray I'd seen when I was on the ferry and I wondered if it was just another dead thing in the ocean now, sinking to the bottom, and the postman drove away slowly, as if he wasn't sure if it was all right to leave me unattended, like I could explode or get kidnapped.

18

It was my last session at the clinic when I began to wonder if my husband was in on it, somehow—the questions, electrodes, blue liquid—if maybe he was on the other side of a mirrored window somewhere, but I didn't remember any mirrored windows, so maybe it was more subtle, maybe he had a lab technician or the lead scientist or the whole team on his side, and it was everyone versus me, an undetectable war against an un-understandable wife, a Trojan horse—this study I'd volunteered for, for the sake of science, a discovery, for the sake of a slightly better understanding of the mess of all minds.

At my last session the man with the black hair and large, soft hands was sliding the cold jelly and electrodes on my scalp as usual. We watched the monitor and he'd move one electrode, trying to get the right feedback, but another one would go off (*Oh, drat*) and the little digits flashing didn't mean anything to me, but one of them would switch from maybe a 2 to a 0 (*Oh, drat*) and he'd worm his fingers through my hair, all matted with the jelly, and push the electrode and I'd feel something shift that was tiny and cool, like the ice-cold foot of a fly (*Oh, drat*), and I looked up at the man with the black hair and the large, soft hands and tried to estimate how well he could lie and whether this whole study was just a long search for what part of me was missing. What had once seemed completely impersonal and routine now seemed invasive and insane—grotesque in how close it let people get into my brain. But, no, of course not, of course not of course not ofcoursenot. This was a study, not a plot. I had signed a form months ago that said this was a *study* and they weren't going to use any of this information in any way that would hurt me and even I would not have access to the information they took and it would all be anonymous and the lab technicians had also taken oaths, I'm sure, and it was all for science, not for my husband, and this was a prestigious university and prestigious people were a part of this work and everyone was playing by the rules and my husband was not a part of it, not in on it, not even close to it and I had no real reason to think that he would or could be because he was also a prestigious person, wasn't he, with his thin hair and serious eyes and chalkboard and the dedication he had to numbers, to finding something that was somehow narrowly hidden in them, and he knew that thing was there, somewhere, in the numbers and similarly I knew (or thought I knew) that something was hidden in my husband and I, too, had to find it, had been looking for it, had wondered if somehow something of Ruby was hidden in him, somehow, if she was folded into him by accident.

Are you ready?

The soft-handed, black-haired man was behind the window (just clear, no mirror) and speaking through the microphone to me.

Yes, I said.

Would you like me to read the rules of the study again?

No, thank you.

All right. We'll begin. What is your earliest memory?

Fireflies, I said, because you were supposed to say whatever came to mind first, no matter what it was, but if it was just one word they would ask the same question again—

What is your earliest memory?

The day my mother brought Ruby home. She was two. I was also two. I don't know if I actually remember this or if I just remember a photograph of this, and my mother was tan and happy looking, like she'd been on vacation, which she had just before picking up Ruby at the orphanage, and she was holding Ruby on her hip and she was smiling but the pictures of my mother bringing me home from the hospital two years before looked like someone had just beaten her up and handed her a baby.

Thank you. Tell me a nightmare you had as a child.

That I'd grow so big overnight that I wouldn't be able to leave my room.

Thank you. Please explain the feeling of love.

Someone holding you by the wrist.

Thank you. What is your happiest memory as an adult?

The summer after Ruby died, being at the park with my husband. The light. We smiled.

Thank you. What do you believe happens when we die?

And I understood that you were supposed to say the first thing that came to mind but nothing actually came to mind in that moment and in fact everything seemed to slip out of mind, and all I could think of was a desert, a canyon, and that didn't seem to have much to do with anything—

What do you believe happens when we die?

More silence.

What do you believe happens when we die?

A desert, a canyon.

Thank you. What is your fondest childhood memory?

Ruby's tenth birthday party. She wore a red dress and we skated and she told me we were halfway to twenty and someday we would go to France. It was also my birthday party. We didn't know her exact birthday, but we guessed it could be maybe the same day as mine.

Thank you. What do you know for sure?

I don't know anything for sure.

Thank you. What is your greatest fear?

I wanted to ask, what exactly did he mean by greatest—largest, most ferocious, grandest, most grandiose, most impossible—but I knew that the content of the questions wasn't supposed to matter and the content of my answers also didn't matter, because they were just studying the way a brain moves, how but not exactly where it goes.

What is your greatest fear?

I did everything wrong.

Thank you. What is the point of love?

To distract us.

Thank you. Is there an afterlife?

The questions kept coming like normal on this last day (for me) of the study and I went to the lab for more blood work and I smiled at the nurse when she smiled at me and I drank the blue liquid, then went to the dark room and I loved the dark room, but when the man asked, *What is the value of travel?* and *What is the most memorable place you have ever visited?*, I wondered for a moment if they knew something about my plans to leave the next week and I began to wonder, again, if my husband was in on all this—and I worried he knew I had the ticket for the next week and I wondered if he'd try to stop me—whether he'd somehow lock me in the apartment or show up at the gate or buy a ticket for the seat next to mine—this is how it would have gone in the soaps, I knew, over-turned chairs, screamed names and vengeance and maybe a curse and often a window punched through and often blood and often a hospital, and in the hos-pital there'd be one kind moment between two lovely, loving people before the IVs were ripped out and beep-ing monitors went flat, a doctor, a *Clear!*, a jolt, but that was for television, for fiction, an exaggeration of what the rest of life was and I remembered my mother watching the soaps, this yellow-tinted memory of my mother behind a cloud of smoke, Ruby sitting at her feet, a forgotten bowl of cereal now lukewarm mush there in their real life, which they weren't a part of in that moment, but now I couldn't remember if this was a memory or a photograph or a total invention be-cause I'd asked my mother once what soap she'd fol-lowed in the eighties and she said she hadn't and didn't know what I was talking about and maybe she was right, but I think she was wrong, and I think that's the thing about fiction, that you live in it totally for a little while but you must forget it, sometimes totally forget it, in order to go about the rest of your life.

When I got home after that last day after the study I had an urge to look through my husband's files extensively, an urge I'd been repeatedly having and repeatedly suffocating because I knew it wasn't nice to snoop around like that. When I finally gave in I actually had no clear idea of what I was even looking for, but I told myself that it didn't matter what I was looking for because the urge was large and serious and it was best just to get out of its way, so I did and I found his mother's death certificate and it didn't say *suicide* in the cause-of-death box, it said *accidental*, and my chest went warm for a moment because my first thought was that my husband had lied so that he could say he'd felt what I'd felt, that he knew what it was like to see a person lose herself to herself, that he'd created a fiction so he could get near the stuff of life that I was in. And if he had lied then what a horrible thing to spend such a long time lying about and what a sick thing to do—but what had probably happened, I assured myself, was that the person who filled out this certificate couldn't find the ability to write the word *suicide* in that box because some people just can't stand to live in a world where people sometimes take themselves out of it by choice and some people need to live in a world where suicides are all some kind of *misunderstanding*, some kind of *accident*, some lie that needs correcting and this reminded me of how at the end of my last morning at the clinic someone had said, *See you next week?* And I said, *Yes.* And I knew I was lying but that someone didn't know I was lying unless that someone knew enough about me now to know when I was lying and if that someone did know that much they still lied right back to me by saying, *Take care*, and that was kind of whoever it was, to let us go on living in a little fiction; sometimes I think I don't get enough of that in life, though other times I think I might get more than my fair share.

19

I sat on a curb in Takaka for a long time, trying to think clearly about mixed feelings.

Being alone was what I wanted; being alone was not what I wanted. I didn't want to want anything; I wanted to want everything. I wanted to want a regular life: the usual husband, the usual apartment, the usual streets, sidewalks, noises, and so on. But I had left it. I had gone elsewhere. That was the right decision, I believed, except when I didn't, which was both often and rarely.

I sat on the curb in Takaka and thought these things.

A tremendous amount of my brain was filled with noticing new things out here where nothing was familiar: buildings, types of cars, types of people, accents, plants, packaged-food items. Before I left my brain never had to register my bedroom, my husband, mailbox, apple core, alarm clock, walls. My brain just said, "—, —, —, —, —, —, —, —," to those things, because a brain lets you keep going, keep not seeing your same walls, underwear, husband, doorknobs, ceiling, husband, husband. A brain can be merciful

in this way: sparing you the monotony of those mo-
notonies, their pitiful cozy. A brain lets all the bore-
filled days shrink like drying sponges until they're
hard and ungiving.

At the same time, I missed my ceiling. I missed
how the drywall by the bathroom was uneven. I missed
hearing the door open, hearing the door close, knowing a familiar body was in the other room, moving
around, going about itself.

I walked into the library and the library smelled
like every library I'd ever been in and Dewey deci-
mals were on all the spines, same tiny font, tiny numbers, and I thought, for a moment, that there actually
were things you could count on in this world until I
realized that the most dependable things in the world
are not of any significant use to any substantial problems. I left the library after some time and I thought I
should maybe bring some groceries or something to
Werner's and I tried to determine if I should hitch
again, but I didn't want to explain myself to anyone
and I thought if I heard someone call me brave one
more time I might rip off my own thumb and not
even bother to stop the blood from staining their
upholstery.

I bought some pears and cashews and canned beans
while thinking about whether a person could be physically capable of tearing off their own thumb and the
specifics of that thought kept me company on the long
walk to Werner's place. When I found him standing
shirtless in his side yard, I was holding the scrap of
paper he'd written his address on that night in New

York, so I let my backpack thud off me and I handed the scrap of paper to him for lack of anything else to do with it.

Ah, yes. That's where we are.

He smiled and I smiled, but only a very little.

So you're here, Werner said. I could tell he meant he hadn't actually expected me to come. Maybe I should have felt a bit of shame or a bit of awkwardness, but I did not, for some reason, because I had some rare confidence in being here, that this was the right place for me to be for an indefinite amount of time, that this was the place where I could maybe make sense to myself.

Well, I should show you around, at least, he said, like I'd just won something he didn't want to give away.

His place was a series of small wooden cabins and recycled trailers connected by unevenly cut doors he had to duck a little to get through. He'd built these semi-ruins himself, a constant project over the last twentysomething years he'd been out here. It's probably a good distraction from living alone, something to schedule a day around, something to give urgency to the unurgent weeks: rusted hinges, peeling caulk, a leak, more peeling, more rust, more leaks—the circular requirements of shelter. He kept the kitchen stocked as if he was waiting for the world to end—a pantry packed with cans, an extra freezer just for cuts of meat and flour sacks. In my bedroom and the living room, he'd raised the trailer ceilings using wooden planks, salvaged windowpanes, and bubble wrap. It brought in a grassy, greenhouse kind of light, but the room still smelled like animal and mildew.

The brain needs space to breathe, he said.

It's nice. There is a lot of air here, I said. Dead bugs lounged on dust pillows in the corner. Gnats buzzed.

We'll have tea at six, he said before he left me in my shed-room, and I was thankful that he didn't try to make sure I was okay, and he didn't ask if I needed anything, and he didn't thank me for bringing those groceries, and this was probably why I was here: that this was one of those places I could go that just didn't count toward anything, time I could be alone and alone with being alone and Werner knew or understood that or maybe he didn't understand but it didn't matter if he knew it or not because whether or not he knew, I believed it was understood.

You decided against bringing the family.

What family? I asked. We were having dinner on the porch that faced the ravine, where we always had dinner, the only time we sat to eat a meal.

Well, he said, head tilted and chewing meat, *I just supposed that you had one. You seem like a part of that kind of machine.*

I don't really have a family, I said.

Well, that would explain why your family isn't here, if they are not in existence.

Werner put his knife down on his dinner plate. I knew he would explain himself in this way, too, that he was without family.

Did you know that lambs lie down to be slaughtered? he asked. *Such sad little creatures they are. So hopeless.*

His sheer hair fluttered. I looked down at the ravine

then up at the sky morphing into blues and purples. I have recalled this night often, sometimes daily, in the years since I left New Zealand, but I still do not know why it is this moment that I remember so clearly—sky, Werner, knife on plate, talk of how lambs die—instead of one of the louder, more eventful ones. Some of the loudest and most eventful events that happened there are still foggy, half-ruined slide shows, the images unfocused, a fleshy thumb obscuring some key thing or person. But that night it seemed I had reached some indescribable reason, and the wildebeest sulked away, and I made some sense to myself and I wouldn't say I was happy or even content, but I had emptied myself of something and was just there.

I eat them for the sake of this pity, Werner said, pushing this dripping bite into his mouth.

What makes them lie down?

Pardon?

I mean, why do they give up so easily?

Werner put another bite of animal in his mouth and chewed.

They are not giving up, he said. *They are just being polite.*

He smiled, then turned back to face the ravine.

I crossed my feet at the ankles, then bent one leg over the other. Something that sounded like a bucket of nails being poured on the tin roof happened, then it went away.

Possums, he said, nodding toward where the noise had come from.

20

The front desk sent flowers and a balloon and a stuffed bear—the string noosed around his neck.

My husband and I watched telenovelas and every few minutes he would translate a good line, though it was obvious what was going on. There were lovers and there were enemies and sometimes you couldn't tell them apart but it hardly mattered. Men tossed their heads around when they spoke. Old ladies cast spells. Doll-perfect women with angry black hair stomped in heels and demanded and demanded and demanded.

And I, like my husband, would rather watch someone else be angry than go through the trouble of my own, so while we watched the women spit and choke each other and the men shout and rub their temples, we felt our own anger dissolve or go numb. We had been angry that the other was angry and even angrier that we were experiencing anger—it was our honeymoon and if we were not exempt from pain now, we might never be.

The pain we were not exempt from had been made visible in the cast around my arm, which was fixing my wrist, maybe, but not us, this cast which was put on at the clinic I'd been carried to after falling down fifteen marble stairs outside our hotel: a twisted ankle, scraped knees, a broken wrist, a bruise, and a gash across my cheek. (*She fell down the stairs*, he said, *I fell down the stairs*, I said, and isn't that what people say has happened when that is exactly what hasn't happened?) In fact, I *had* fallen down the stairs as we were arguing, or as we were trying not to argue and failing deeply. We had just checked in to this hotel, smiling and overpronouncing *gracias* and *bueno* and when the clerk had cooed, *Oh, the honeymoon suite!*, my husband put his hand on my shoulder and looked at me and I don't know exactly why, but I looked at my husband and pretended I had no idea what was going on, and he said, *What was that all about?* And I said, *What?* And he said, *Back there at reception—your, I don't know, your attitude, it's just not like you* and this took us into a conversation about attitudes and about what I was usually *like*, and this conversation tried its best not to be an argument, and we tried our best to be the sweet, sense-making people we had mostly been up to this moment, through the all-smiles, all-talking, all-consuming wave of the wedding, but this discussion of attitudes eventually fell into the argument category and we argued up the elevator, into the honeymoon suite, through the bathroom door, back into the hallway, back down the elevator, through the lobby, and back outside the hotel and I got a little distracted by this obscenely attractive Spanish woman walking beside us as my husband was saying, *Elyria, it's like this, you have two options*—and I was thinking, *Fuck you so much, Husband, it's not like that and I have a lot more than two options*—and this was what was in my head when I missed that first step and began the tumble, which just seemed so deeply appropriate, such a good end to our argument about attitudes and the two options I supposedly had and what I was usually *like*. And after the fall as I was splayed and shocked at the bottom of the stairs, a sturdy bellhop was the first to reach me—*Señorita, señorita*—and my husband was the second person to reach me, but it was too late because the bellhop was already scooping me up and carrying me the few blocks to the little clinic and all my husband could do was trail along behind us, he and his *It's like this* and his *You have two options*.

That night, what was supposed to be a romantic dinner became a silent dinner.

I stared, nauseated, at the paella, which seemed putrid, spoiled. I ran the edge of a fork along a gaping mussel shell stabbed in the rice, and I considered picking up a knife for no good reason, but I did not pick up the knife because I knew I would have likely been unable not to stab the ciabatta out of its stupid basket and fling it across the restaurant, so I didn't pick up the knife because I knew that throwing anything during the middle of a romantic-turned-silent dinner was not appropriate and would create more problems than the satisfaction of stabbing and throwing something would have given.

My husband was staring at me with this brand-new look of his, one I had never seen before but would see much more of in the future; he was looking at me like I was a very nice thing of his that wasn't working quite like it should, like he'd found a defect, a defect that was extremely disappointing because he had spent a lot of time doing his research and believed he had gotten a thing that was guaranteed against these kinds of defects, and maybe there was some kind of *glitch* in the system and maybe he needed to have a professional *assess* the situation, give him an estimate.

I looked at him, extremely silent, and I wanted to say, *Husband, I dare you, I dare you to*—but I didn't know what I was daring him to do, just that I was daring him—*I dare you, I dare you*—and I wondered about how many other sides of him I had not yet seen and that was exciting in a way and terrifying in a way and I didn't want to feel both excited and terrified right then—I just wanted to feel calm, to feel like a sedated animal on a honeymoon, or to feel like a drunk and beautiful Spanish woman, but I was not drunk or beautiful or Spanish and I wondered if there was a side of my husband who wanted to demolish me, who wanted to turn me into a fine dust, who would bring his solid hands against my throat, who would rend my muscles from the bone without a flinch, in a moment of passion, if he had that kind of passion in him, if that kind of passion was quietly growing in him like an undiscovered tumor. And if so, did I have that tumor, too? Was there some part of me that would rip his arm off his body if I was given the chance and ability? And if I did have that part of me would it be the kind of thing that just healed on its own? Was it a broken-rib thing? The kind of thing you can't do a damn thing about but try not to cough or laugh for a few months? Maybe I should try to just hold still for a year or so, I thought, and this feeling would mend itself—unless this wasn't a broken-rib kind of thing but more like an internal-bleeding kind of thing and maybe this bleeding was going to rot us from the inside, hot blood swishing around into corners of us that it should never be. Or maybe it was nothing and I was overreacting and I should just be who I was expected to be—be the senseful and just fine and reliable woman who had fallen in love with my husband and whom my husband had fallen in love with—I could be her, I thought, and I inhaled and exhaled and was pretty sure that it was all just fine.

Is everything okay? Aren't you hungry?

He looked at me hard in the eye, the way an optometrist would.

21

On *occasion*, Werner said as we watched the color drain from the sky on one of those repeated nights, *I consider three possibilities for the world. One, the women have it worse. Two, the men have it worse. Or three, everyone has it equally bad.*

This was a few weeks into my stay at Werner's. We had established a safe routine of staying out of each other's way, though sometimes we'd end up standing in the kitchen at the same time having tea and toast, not speaking. Once he brought in a few clippings of lemon verbena, put them on the kitchen table, and said, *It's lemon verbena*, and I just nodded. After I'd done to the garden what I could do to the garden I'd go walk in the woods or hitchhike to town to release the impulse to buy something, to have a coffee or a beer or to consider going but never actually go to the library to send an email to my husband, to let him know I was fine and not to worry, not to bother worrying because there was nothing to worry about anymore and I was fine with my new, tiny life of just a few words and a few people and plants.

And, Werner continued, *it is not often that I have a*

*female mind to consult about these possibilities and so, I
bring this question to your attention, if you will attend it.*

*Men have it worse . . . women have it worse . . . or no
one has it worse?*

*These are the options we can consider. This is my ri-
diculous game for us to speak of, here, as we view the
ravine.*

*We should establish categories, I said, and assign points
to each category depending on how important that category
is to overall life happiness. There should be a winner for
each one. We should keep score.*

That seems fair.

After debating and assigning points, then tallying
them up while the possums scrambled in the darkness around us, we agreed that men had it better.

Weeks vanished. In the garden I was a thing with a
particular use: pumpkin-vine waterer, bean-stalk trim-
mer, tomato-root coverer. I was suddenly essential.
The pumpkins would shrivel without me. The toma-
toes would die of thirst. The summer would have
sunned them dead.

After dinner I read or did nothing and sometimes
in the morning I swam in the muddy bay, backstrok-
ing to nowhere and coming back to where I'd started.
At night I slept on a thin, knotty mattress and had
dreams that were never about operating a dishwasher.
And I began to believe that you could exchange your
life, send it back for a different model, and I knew
that wasn't really true but I also knew that it wasn't,
here, entirely untrue.

And I did not fold fitted sheets or meet deadlines or go to the grocery store or do our taxes or call 1-800 numbers to complain. I did not wear electrodes or answer questions.

I did not hear my husband opening the front door or closing the front door.

And I did not feel guilt; I did not feel guilty; I forgot all the things that could have caused any warm ounce of that feeling.

Werner was standing in the kitchen struggling with the lid on a jar of orange marmalade, his face compressing and filling with blood. He looked up and put the jar on the counter, scraped something out of the sink, and tossed it out the window. The population of flies seemed to have tripled overnight and they circulated in the kitchen, more active and audible than usual; when I tried to brush one away, it would stay, indignant, on my skin or fly a tiny circle and return to the same spot.

I picked up the marmalade and opened it with a pop. We stood and ate jagged slices of toast with the marmalade and Werner didn't say anything about how I had opened the jar, but as I was about to head back down to the garden Werner broke the silence, saying, *You are a strange creature.* A curd of orange marmalade was on his chin. I focused on the curd of marmalade.

I didn't want to say anything because I liked how, until now, we never spoke in the morning.

You aren't doing anything in particular here, are you?
What do you mean?

You don't appear to have any plans.

I don't want to have plans, I said.

Werner's mouth turned slowly to a frown.

But where will you go next?

He took a large bite of toast and stared in a way that made me severely uncomfortable and I tried to hide my severe discomfort and I wanted to tell him that this *was* my plan, to come here and stay here, because life was simple and I could be useful for a place to stay and not be near my husband and not be near my past and not think about time or plans or deadlines or that rust spot in my old shower that bothered me so much or that wild animal with all the teeth charging toward me called the future, and in the months I'd been here my wildebeest had shut up and I did not want to provoke the wildebeest because it had been so long that it had been silent, but I knew I couldn't explain that to him, explain to him that a large and useless and angry animal was in me—

I haven't thought about what's next . . . It's just being here, alone.

But you're not alone here, Elyria. I was alone before you got here but not now—and really, you're one of those people who needs people. You're not meant to be alone.

I wanted to throw a plate at his face, but I did not throw a plate or a whole stack of plates at his face. I said, *Oh, I don't know about that*, and I looked at my feet and I poured half a cup of hot tea down my throat.

No, you are not a happy person alone, I can tell. You come to a country where you could be alone in four thou-

sand ways, yet you choose to have company, to go to the one
place you know a person will be.

I need to finish something in the garden, I said, and I
left and I went down to the garden and I walked in
circles and realized I had nothing to do there so I
hiked up to the highway and went to town and sat on
a bench reading the Katherine Mansfield stories that
I'd borrowed from Werner (who couldn't *make* me
leave, couldn't *make* me) and I read until it was dark
because I didn't want to talk about plans with Werner
and I didn't want to think about plans by myself because I didn't have any and wouldn't make any because
there weren't any to be made—I was here. I was staying here. I wasn't leaving. There was no reason to leave.
So I put my brain elsewhere and when it got dark I
realized that all the bars and cafés were full of people
who had been becoming more and more exuberant
and loud and drunk, and I looked through a window
into one and there were people dancing against each
other and smiling and drinking and they were all wearing Santa hats: women wearing Santa hats, old men in
Santa hats, flimsy-legged boys with thick dreadlocks
wearing Santa hats, and why did they want to imper-
sonate someone who only gives and disappears? What
did they have to give each other?

On the porch of one of the quiet cafés there was a
woman with a long grey braid at a table by herself.
Seeing her alone made me wonder if Jaye was alone
with her family, if she had one of those families that
being with is worse than being alone and maybe that
was why she had invited me to her home for Christmas,

to have an ally in that fight. I felt a slice of guilt, ate and digested it, then forgot about Jaye. I went up and ordered a beer from the window and I sat at a table near the woman with the grey braid and she looked over at me and smiled and said, *It's Christmas again, my dear. Where does the time go?* And she looked up at the tree branches but the tree branches did not answer her, but if they had they would have said that time goes to sleep, it goes insane, it goes on vacation, it goes to Milwaukee, it goes and goes and goes and keeps going, going, gone. Or maybe time is more like a person walking down a street carrying two grocery bags and a grate gives way and that person and their groceries fall to the bottom of the sewer, suddenly elsewhere, suddenly a bloody mess with eggs cracked and splattered and milk spilled because everyone walks around thinking nothing is going to happen right up to the moment when something does happen, just like time, how it's here one minute and we don't notice it till it's gone—no, it's not like that, I would tell the tree branches if I was the type of person who talked to tree branches or imagined a monologue for a tree's branches—no, time is a thing that is always almost a thing that is never here and never gone and never yours and never anyone's and we're all trying to get a hand clutched tight around time and no one ever will, so can't we call a truce, now, Time? I am not asking, I am just saying—I'm calling a truce with time. Truce.

When I got back to Werner's, so late it was early, all the lights were out and I knew Werner probably didn't know if I was home or not and probably didn't care and so I said, *See? I'm fine here. It's like I'm not even here*— And I was talking to Werner but he didn't hear because he wasn't there, wasn't listening, but I was actually talking to myself, or to my whole life but my whole life wasn't listening to me either and my whole life, at that moment, was a garden with no wildebeest tracks in it, not yet, but there was a wildebeest in the forest nearby, I knew, and if I left this calm place I wouldn't be safe and I just needed to figure out a way to explain this to Werner without really explaining it to Werner, because I'd be fine if I could keep staying here, still and goal-less and husbandless and pastless and peopleless, because when I was here I was both here and not here—I was a person made of things that were fine, no wildebeests, just tomato plants and pumpkin vines and mulch made of seaweed and dirt, a pure piece of earth.

The next morning I didn't mean to say what I said to Werner at breakfast, and I don't even know why I was talking, but now I believe that everyone actually does say what they want to say, even when they say, *That's not what I meant, that's not what I meant to say.* A person can only say things that are already in there, waiting for a way out, animals grown sick of fences, and I later wondered if my wildebeest had grown sick of its fence and was ready to migrate even though I wasn't, but my wildebeest didn't listen to me, didn't care what I wanted or what I thought I wanted because the wildebeest was above want, is still above want, is the heaviest thing in me, the thing that still makes all too many choices— That morning I said a phrase I didn't think I could say anymore:

My husband—

And I paused, inhaled deep, realized I hadn't spoken those words in a month or more, and recognized a certain look on Werner's face, a look I had seen on the faces of certain other men when I first mentioned my husband—

. . . told me that you sleep more just before and just after making important progress in your work, creatively, I mean, your creative work.

We didn't say anything for a few seconds.

He's a mathematician, I said.

You said you didn't have a husband.

I only said I didn't have a family.

Werner nodded as if I had just told him the punch line to a riddle. We were holding mugs of tea too hot to drink. I held mine close so the steam put sweat on my face.

What does your husband think about you staying in the center of no place at all with an old man you've only met once?

He was smiling as if this was another part of the riddle, but I knew the answer to this wasn't going to make me look like a particularly nice person. Possibly it was too late for niceness. I started to say something but wasn't sure what to say, so I shut my lips again and I nodded and tried to smile a little. A husband—ha.

He actually doesn't know exactly where I am.

Where does this husband believe his wife has gone?

It isn't exactly clear, I said.

And how long will this wife let this husband be uncertain of her whereabouts?

I've been trying to understand a way to understand that.

Werner tilted his head to the side like there was some nice music playing.

Oh, Miss Elyria. Whatever has gotten into a person like you? Whatever is it that makes a person do a thing like this?

There was no way to answer that question and I'm not the kind of person who tries to explain a thing that has no explanation so I went to the garden and I pulled things out of it, until I could feel the sun putting color on my scalp, until the muscles in my back were twitching in little fits, until the weeds were all wilted in a heap, and all I could think was how there would be more weeds tomorrow and wouldn't it be easier for the world if everything just stayed still, just stopped growing altogether? Maybe it would, but we won't do that, we won't stop, plants don't, people don't, we keep showing up and living and trying to do something and dying and what was it that all these vines and leaves were struggling toward year after century after eternity? Because, really, they would be strangled dead by another weed or else scorched to death or frozen to death or eaten by possums or bugs or people. And I also wondered what it was that had gotten into me, or a person like me, and I wondered what it was that made me do these things, leave my life so abruptly, and I didn't know then what it was because I couldn't know then what I was and I barely know now what it was or still is that made me leave. I think brains might be machines that turn information into feelings and feelings back into decisions and I've discovered that my machine has been put together in a strange way and it translates life in a strange way but I have no way to fix this—I'm not a brain-machine fixer, I'm just a haver of a brain, like anyone, and none of us know how to fix ourselves, at least not entirely, not well enough.

Now I know how to sit still, how to accomplish my job, how to walk home, how to order a sandwich at the diner, how to pay a bill, how to sleep in a cold bed, but I still don't know how to fix my brain, make it turn life information into calm feelings, responsible actions. I know, now, how to ignore everything, how to not talk to strangers, how to not get on one-way planes to countries where I don't belong and that's all I can expect of myself these days, but back then that was all beyond me, that was life at a level that I wasn't able to reach.

I managed to stay completely out of Werner's way for a few days—waking early to work, staying in town all day and sneaking in late, but on that last morning he came down to the garden while I was working and it was clear I had lost my use to him.

You are a sad person, he said, *and I'm not a person who can tolerate other people's sadness.*

I'm not sad.

It's very clear that you are.

Maybe you're projecting. I'm a happy person. I am fine.

I'm not a projector. I am twice your age. I know sadness. Yours is inextricable. It is terminal. I know these things.

I didn't say anything.

It's okay, he finally said. *I get it. You're trying to find yourself.*

I don't want to find myself, I said, but I don't think he heard me.

Who understands what has gotten into women these days—trying to find themselves somewhere, like they've split in two and they're chasing the other part. You're one of those women who thinks nothing is good enough for you, the entire human experience is not good enough for you and you want something impossible.

I didn't say anything but my face must have.

I'm sorry, he said in a tone that said he wasn't actually sorry. *It's really time you left.*

22

Werner—

   I am asking you to remove yourself from my automobile.

I was still. I stayed in my seat.

   Werner, this is ridiculous, you know I don't have anywhere else to go.

Werner took the keys out of the ignition, got out of the car, opened the trunk, and put my backpack on the sidewalk, gently, as if it was living, then he got back into the car.

   Remove yourself from my automobile.

It was hard not to take it personally, how fast he drove away.

A man sitting on the library steps waved as if he'd been expecting me to show up. I looked at him and half-waved back, but then he realized that we didn't know each other so he shrugged and turned back to talk to the man sitting beside him.

Light left the sky quickly when a fat cloud came. A yellow phone booth across the road was so bright, I wondered if it had just been painted.

It was possible, I thought, that my husband had simply replaced me after I left him, that he had simply

gone out and found another woman, a simple fix for
his wifeless life. Someone to understand his situation,
to understand his needs as a human man in this world.
I thought of my husband sitting on a bench looking at
the river down the way. I thought of him running in
the snow. I thought of him eating an apple and how
his jaw could stretch out almost like a snake's, fitting
a whole half of it in his mouth, then he'd chew for a
full five minutes as he clacked at his blackboard.
Across, across, across, and pause, then across some
more, next line, more acrossing. I could see him exactly as he had been on that night months before (a
Tuesday, I think) when I had gone to bed early but I
woke up in the middle of the night, got out of bed for
a glass of water, and stopped at the doorway of his office to look at him writing on his blackboard, clacking away at it like he was some kind of machine, and
as I watched him doing his calculations it occurred to
me that I did love him and that despite loving him I
was still leaving and isn't that what people always roll
their eyes at, say, *That doesn't make sense*, say, *It's mis-
guided, selfish, stupid*, whatever. The little lamp in the
corner of my husband's office made his fair skin seem
golden and he smiled at me and I thought this was how
I would always remember him. This is the little piece
of my husband that I will store permanently in myself.

Did it wake you? Am I working too loudly?

No, I like it. It's a good noise.

I thought you hated the chalkboard.

*I do, but the sound of you putting things on it makes it
okay.*

I know that when other memories of my husband have gone threadbare and splintered, this will be the one that lives. When I am eighty and explaining my life to someone much younger I will pause when I mention my first marriage and this will be the version of my husband that I remember. Smiling his tiny smile, his I-am-in-the-middle-of-something-but-I-love-you smile.

Remembering this, I put myself inside that phone booth and didn't expect him to answer, or if he did I was expecting not to recognize his voice, like he might be using a new one by now. But that didn't happen. He answered. He said hello like there had been no change in his life, like his life had gone on completely and normally without me being around, like he could just keep waking up and having coffee and clacking at the blackboard and jogging in the park and saying the same words in the same way and sleeping on the same side of the bed and making the same steaks in his skillet and turning on the lights in the same bedroom when the sun went down and reading a book in his same reading chair and all the while his voice wouldn't get up and leave his throat and his body wouldn't take itself apart and fall into a little heap on the floor and his brain wouldn't turn to mud and pour out of his ears. He could do all the things that he did when I was there, even when he was doing those things without me being there.

Hello, he said.

Hello? he said.

I said his name.

I said, *It's Elyria.*

He said, *Ha.*

Then we were quiet for I don't know how long. A big truck drove by. The man who was driving was hooting at the radio, the sound of a crowd cheering.

I went to New Zealand.

I know.

And I should have told you.

My husband inhaled fast, tried to make a word and didn't.

Well? he asked.

Well, what?

Do you have something to say?

I don't know.

You don't know.

I'm not sure.

He did the inhale thing again. *Well, if it's all the same to you I'm going to get back to work now. The next time you call you might want to have something to say.*

And the line went dead and a machine woman started speaking, asking for more money, saying, *Please,* saying, *Have a nice day.*

I slung my backpack on, walked down an alley, put my backpack down, and crouched over it to have an almost-human moment. I felt like I got close to being a rational person right then, phlegm dripping in my throat, face turning red. In this situation, any rational person would be hurt, would feel lost, and being hurt and feeling lost would cause her to do a real thing, to really cry. A rational person would feel upset instead of just knowing she was upset. Her feelings would show up in her body as if she had no choice in the matter and this would cause her to realize she needed to find a way back to her home, to her real life that was somehow going on without her. She would immediately go to an airport and buy a plane ticket. She would start practicing her apologies on the flight and when she got back home she would start seeing a therapist to prove to herself and everyone else how sorry she was, how wrong she was, how much she needed help. And if she was lucky, her husband would work hard to forgive her—he would work at forgiveness every day like it was an extremely difficult equation. And slowly, eventually, they would go back to being okay, to being a two-piece team moving through life. And when this rational person was in therapy she would talk about things like her dead sister and her monster mother—and where the hell *was* her father, anyway?—and through all this she would make progress in her therapy and when someone asked how she was she would say, *I am okay; I'm in therapy; we're sorting things out; we're making progress.* But first this rational person would need to get to an airport and buy a plane ticket straight back home and before she could do that she would need to have the courage to do that and before she could have the courage she would need to want to have the courage, to need to want to try to have the courage to say, *I give up, I was wrong, take me home.*

In my almost-human moment, I felt the tears building up behind my eyes, bubbling there, humming like a teakettle before it boils, but I didn't cry. Blood rushed around in my body like it was being chased, but then it stopped—maybe it realized there is nowhere for blood to go but around and around and as I thought this I knew I wasn't always a rational person, or even a nice one. I stood up straight, put myself back in order, and tried to figure out where to go next.

23

He said the night terrors had never happened before me and I could never decide if that was comforting or not comforting, if it meant I brought the worst out in him or if it just meant that the majority of my husband was a mostly nice thing—and maybe the realest part of my husband was unaffiliated with the screaming, violent version that shook us both awake some nights. Still, I couldn't forget that there was a distinct possibility that it was me and the way I handled or not quite handled my wifehood that had unhinged this part of him. I had disrupted him. I was the catalyst that began the bad in his life, and I would continue to be a long series of disruptions to him and I was always going to bring out his ugliest side, and my sleeping beside him would always stop him from being able to really *sleep*.

In the early months the night terrors just made sleeping a kind of roulette and there was something perversely satisfying about waking up to his frayed screaming (when life seemed more like a soap opera and less like a life) but that was before the choking began, before the nights his hands would creep across my collarbone and tighten around my neck, and though it usually only took a few small hits to his chest or face to make him stop, a few nights I had to hit him harder than what seemed safe and though he never shut my trachea long enough for me to pass out he sometimes came close, pressing down for a moment, a wink in my throat. When he slipped out of a terror, eyes still shut and jaw slack, he'd fall limp back to his side of the bed and sometimes he'd go immediately back to sleep, and on those nights I'd get out of bed, shaking with adrenaline, and go to the living room couch with my neck bent against the armrest, chin on chest, mind on husband, eyes on window, waiting for some kind of sign, some kind of evidence, some kind of kindness or understanding to tell me, *Self, it is all fine and okay. Close your eyes. Tomorrow it will all be fine.* But I never have been the kind to keep a back-stock of that kind of kindness, the way that other people do, taking care of themselves and others, being ready to forgive.

Other nights, my husband would stay awake and we'd play out the same script:

Did it happen?

Yes.

Elly, my God, Elly, I'm so sorry. Elyria.

And he'd wrap over me and my throat would feel rug burned where he'd twisted the skin.

Elly, talk to me.

But what was there to talk about? What could I say? I had seen how a corner of my husband wanted to stop all the air in me.

Go back to sleep, I'd say.

What was it like this time?

The same.

Did I hurt you?

No. Let's go back to sleep.

This looks like it hurt, Elly.

He'd drag a limp finger over the red lines his hands had left.

I'm fine. We're fine.

And he'd keep staring, waiting for me to say what I knew he needed to hear, something I said so much I wondered why he didn't just say it for me after a while.

I'd say, *I know you didn't mean to.*

I knew that he didn't mean to, or I think I knew he didn't mean to, or it was better to believe that he didn't mean to, but I wondered how I knew, for certain, that he didn't mean to, or if a more accurate thing to say would be that I *trusted* that he didn't mean to, but if I actually did *trust* that he didn't mean to, I should have just said that I *knew* he didn't mean to, which I obviously didn't know for certain since I would stay awake for the rest of the night wondering how I could know, for certain, that he didn't mean to, and what did my lack of certainty mean about how much I trusted or did not trust my husband, about how well or not well our marriage was going, the possibility that we each wanted to cause severe damage to the other, and there was the fact that the only way I could defend my husband's night terrors was to believe that they were an entirely separate phenomenon from him, but I also knew that was incredibly unlikely or actually impossible because my husband was mostly his mind and I believed his mind was what made the night terrors happen. And it's still unclear to me why a person has abilities that they do not want to have, why a person feels things that person doesn't want to feel and why that person doesn't feel things that person does want to feel, and why a person falls out of love when being in love was such a good thing to be in, and why a person makes loud and clumsy attempts at midnight to kill the life one could reasonably expect that person to want to preserve.

So after I said, as I always said, that I knew my husband didn't *mean* to scream and choke me in his sleep (except without saying the words *scream* or *choke* because hearing those words was almost worse than him actually doing those things) we'd lie awake awhile, each pretending to be asleep or almost asleep but we'd always stay up, slipping in and out of sleep for all those hours, each of us moving as little as possible, trying to breathe like we were deeply content, like it would be easy to go back to sleep as soon as we were truly ready, as soon as we were prepared to will ourselves back into the shut-lid place where those terrors lived. But we always avoided talking about these things— difficult things—and I wondered if that meant we'd be a little uncomfortable with or disappointed by each other for the rest of our lives.

Then there was that night when we were arguing about something that didn't matter, something that can be summarized as I Believe You Are a Little More Despicable Than Me, and my husband wasn't listening to me and I wasn't listening to my husband but we were making our arguments at the same time in low voices, and I picked up the glass of neat bourbon that he'd bought for me like this was a date instead of what it was: a married couple's attempt to pretend to be in a marriage that was the kind of marriage where we went out on things like dates, but instead became a married couple's chance to argue, as discreetly as possible, in public, and I picked up that glass of bourbon that he'd bought for me and I started to lift it to my mouth before I thought of splashing it into my husband's face, but I didn't want to do that—I didn't want to give or do anything to my husband because I didn't want to acknowledge that my husband was even a person in my life, so I poured the glass of bourbon onto the table and when I poured it onto the table I didn't mean to say that it wasn't nice of him to have bought it for me and I didn't mean to say that it didn't taste good or that I was already drunk enough; what I meant was I am a liquid and he is a solid and the universe is expanding and here we go flying away from each other like matter always does, spinning and spilling off the edge of our table and onto our laps.

This put an end to whatever we were fighting about.

We stared into the puddle of nice bourbon, a round, amber shimmer, and we looked up and around the bar to see if anyone had seen me do this and we tried to laugh a little about it and I told my husband that I would write this into one of the episodes of the soap opera someday and he kept laughing for a beat but then he stopped laughing—

You would do that?

I thought I detected a bit of wonder in his voice, that he'd like to become part of a story, any story.

Yeah, of course.

You would take something of ours and turn it into a scene?

I'd exaggerate it, of course. It wouldn't be the same.

What do you mean?

It would have to be so much more dramatic to make it onto the show. I mean, to those characters a twelve-dollar glass of bourbon is nothing—someone would have to pour a really good bottle of Scotch on the table. Something rare.

I guess so, he said.

As we walked home that night smelling like the bourbon that had drizzled onto our knees, I knew that my husband was a song that I had forgotten the words to and I was a fuzzy photograph of someone he used to love and I also knew that the song that my husband was, the song I had forgotten, was not only forgotten but no longer existed, that there had only been one record of it and it had been melted down and turned into something else and only one person knew how to sing it and that person was long since dead. My husband and I were no longer the people that fit easily into each other's life, but we suggested those people, and this was why I would often catch him looking at me as if I merely looked familiar to him. We did not exist, the *we* we thought we'd always be.

24

On the ferry back to the North Island I sat at the bar
because the tender tender was there and I tried to not
be disappointed that she didn't seem to remember me.
I read Mrs. Bridge again, or, rather, just moved my eyes
over the words and wondered where I was going or
what I should do now or how I was going to find a way
to disappear my wildebeest. I thought of the first time
I saw the tender tender and remembered the halo of
the inaudible noise I heard back then and I felt compelled by it, but also suspicious of it, and there was a
dissonance, between the inaudible noise and the sus-
picion, a long chord in a minor key. I didn't know if
I would call Jaye or not call Jaye, if going to Napier
would be worth the trouble, if anywhere was worth
the trouble. I watched the tender tender moving around,
pouring pints and prying caps until she leaned down
on the bar, head propped in hands, to watch a staticky
TV. A police rendering of a woman was on the screen,
then a second and a third version, each with slight
variations, the different ways that witnesses had remembered her. Her eyes slightly larger in this one;
a longer nose in that. There were no photographs of

her, the television said—this woman had avoided photographs her whole life.

You know what she did, don't you?

She kill somebody? the man said.

Tried to, the tender tender said. *Tried to kill her husband. Killed her little girl's pet rabbit and set the neighbor's house on fire.*

She did, did she?

Aye, she did. She left her husband tied up and covered with rabbit blood.

Someone said once that they'd never heard of a crime they couldn't imagine committing, and I realized then that if I had a daughter and she had a rabbit and that rabbit was alone with me and I was feeling the way I felt right now and I had a way to kill that rabbit and the time to spend killing that rabbit then killing the rabbit was something I could imagine myself possibly doing or at least considering doing or being on the edge of doing. And smearing a husband with the blood wasn't such a far step after that if you had a desire to smear your husband with blood and smearing someone with blood was something I could imagine a situation calling for because there were at least a few people in this world that I wouldn't not like to see smeared with blood—one person being Werner for fucking my plans, for sending me back out into a life with my wildebeest, to figure out a way to live here and I didn't want to do that and I didn't know how to do that and I wasn't sure how I was going to do that—

A man sitting beside me leaned over and said, *Ya travelin'?*

It took me a second to get back into this place, this boat where I was floating between islands and not setting a house on fire and smearing a person with blood, but I somehow said, *Yes, I am.*

The man was somewhere between attractive and haggard, like he'd been a stunt double for a classic movie star but had been beaten up a few too many times.

I saw you get outta a car by the station—hitching?

I didn't like that he'd made a dotted line between the person I'd been an hour ago and the person I was now.

Yeah, have been, I said.

American?

Yeah.

I'll tell you something—and I don't say this to upset you, just to make you think—there was this American girl here about this time last year and she'd been hitching about, getting from here to there, you know. Maybe it had been a few months of this and she'd been doing just fine until this bloke picked her up round Christchurch and he chopped her up into about fifty-five pieces and left her all over the country.

He wasn't looking at me as he spoke. We both watched the tender tender, our patron saint.

All right, I said. *Well. Thanks for letting me know.*

I don't say it to make you stop what you're doing, but just so you know it's not the smartest thing you could do and you should watch out—you know, think about what you're doing. Don't get into the car with someone who looks like they might be able to chop you up.

No one can make decisions based on hypothetical knife skills, I didn't say.

You Americans are always saying how you come here and don't want to leave but I don't think you mean dead and chopped up, you know? That's not what you mean.

I'd never said anything about not leaving.

The tender tender came over, looked at my glass, and looked at me and that was all she needed to know to fill it to the rim again and, oh, dear God, I will love her every day for the rest of forever.

25

For at least an hour I just walked up and down the same few blocks in Wellington, thinking about hitching up to Napier to see Jaye, and when I thought of Jaye I would hear the inaudible noise but then the minor chord would start and the dissonance would begin and I would walk back the other way, think of calling Dillon or going to a hostel, and the inaudible noise would gain volume over the minor chord, and I would decide against Dillon or a hostel, then start walking toward the highway again until the minor chord came back, and this went and went for a while, my pacing—noise, chord, dissonance, noise—but finally my thumb caught a car before my mind could change and when I got to Napier I got out of the car downtown and I found a pay phone and called the number Jaye had given me so many weeks earlier. It rang and rang and no one answered and nothing happened so I hung up and watched the passing cars. They went by slowly, calmly, all stopping at the stop sign, taking their turn to do what they should do until one car sped past the stop sign and hit another car in the intersection and that car tried to swerve but jumped a curb and ran into a building and a window shattered right out of it. A man started shouting, then ran up to the pay phone and dialed and yelled and I started thinking about the time that Ruby called me in the middle of the day to ask me to come over to her apartment and when I got there she was frying bacon, frying it one slice at a time, putting it on a plate then sitting and eating it, then getting up and frying another slice. She finished a whole package that afternoon and I didn't know whether to be amazed or afraid, amazed or afraid—I couldn't choose which to be and neither one was happening naturally and what was I to make of it, all this bacon eating? The other car had spun a circle and was now hip to hip with a parked car, squeezed together like a picture of friends. Steam or smoke leaked from the car hood, and was I amazed or afraid? I couldn't get a grasp on a feeling and I kept thinking of Ruby putting slick slices of bacon in her mouth. Her eyes seemed foggy and far-off and I remembered that she had endured a childhood not unlike mine but also very unlike mine, this woman who was my sister, but only legally, this person who'd emerged on the other side of the world, the product of some strangers' bodies, this woman with whom I'd endured the same parents—*who was she?* Bacon turned itself into her body, thickened her blood with lipids.

I'm depressed, she said, *and I'm thinking of my mother.*
You mean the one you don't know?
Yes, the one I don't know.
What about her?

I saw something lower in Ruby's face, something drain out of her.

What about her? she repeated, squinting.

I tried to look at Ruby with some kind of tenderness but I think it came out as condescension and I couldn't feel my face, I couldn't feel my face wrapped around my head, and I couldn't feel the muscles in it and make them move in the right way. I was trapped in my body and Ruby was trapped in her body and we'd always been trying to bridge the difference between our bodies, atone for the fact that we were supposed to be family but we weren't, not really, but we had to try anyway, try forever over and over again to find the way that we were related.

I think my mother ate a lot of pork, Ruby finally said, *while she was pregnant with me.*

We'd both been staring out the window and into an apartment across the street. A woman in a peach dress was pacing, pointing a remote control at some unseen device.

I sometimes get this way, Elly, it's like someone else is in my brain, telling me what to do. I go out. I buy a pound of bacon. I come home and eat the whole thing. I feel like I can hear her voice. I know it's stupid, it's crazy, it's whatever, but it's how I feel—I really hear it.

Her expression was broad and placid, like an ocean while no wind is blowing, and a few months later Ruby did not exist anymore, and years later I was standing on a sidewalk in another country, thinking of that moment, still trying to find a feeling about it and trying to find a feeling about these wrecked cars—afraid or amazed? I wandered away from the cars as a crowd grew. An ambulance was singing. I walked with the setting sun at my back, hoping to find the ocean. I thought of Ruby and the dust that danced in light beaming from the window. She curled around her belly packed full of dead pig, packed full of the need she had to hear her mother's voice.

I had barely spoken all day, but I couldn't tell whether I missed that flank of myself, my voice, and I thought of the inaudible noise and when I thought of it, it was there, and it filled the vacuum left by my voice and I wondered if the shadow of the inaudible noise was the same thing as the inaudible noise itself, if I actually needed to be near Jaye for it to last or if it could exist without her, if it could live entirely in the memory of her, or if, instead, I needed direct exposure to Jaye to keep generating it, a vitamin-D kind of thing—and the sun went down and there was nowhere for me to be: no destination, no stranger offering a home or car and there was no way for anyone to reach me, to find me, to call me, to tell me anything, and I was fully alone, leashed within my utter self. The ocean mumbled somewhere east of me, and I could hear it but I couldn't see it, that black ocean floating in the black air, whispering salt into any open ear. On a street corner, a child was standing like a sad statue, staring off, and as I got closer to him I began to distinctly feel worry—where did he belong and who did he belong to and what would happen to him if he had been forgotten or misplaced, if he wandered like a stray animal through alleyways and under highway bridges and along creekbeds on the edge of town? When I came closer to him a smile flickered on his face, small muscles twitching, like a lightbulb shorting out. He was holding what I thought was a juice box but it turned out to be a pack of cigarettes.

Are you okay? I said.

Are you *okay?* he said, then we both said nothing, and he turned and ran down the block, crawled under a bush on the edge of a garden. It shook as he went through it and then it stopped shaking and I waited for the sound of a door shutting or to see a light in the house turn on or to hear some voice, some sense that he was okay, but there was nothing and there was a possibility that someone might later slice him out of existence and even though I knew that he wouldn't be fine forever, I wanted to have a sense of his security right then, and I knew it would be a false sense of security, but at least it would be a sense of security, but I kept walking toward the ocean, trying to remind myself that before I had seen the boy he had been existing just fine without my worry and I turned a corner and the midnight ocean was there, all sudden and massive. The coast was all smooth, grey oval rocks and I trudged through it to get closer to the ocean, overcome by the sound of it, the blue-grey arc where it met the navy sky. The ocean sighed and moaned and sighed. I sat down, the weight of my pack burrowing me slightly into the rocks, and I listened to the ocean's sighs and thought of my husband's sighs, his tiny sighs and the story he once told me of the year he spent religious while he was working for a nonprofit that tried to feed and clothe the shoeless, ball-bellied, sunken-eyed children of far-off countries.

A seagull walked up and looked at me as if we had known each other for years so I should know exactly what he was thinking and I'd never seen a seagull out walking in the dark, but then the seagull limped away. I found myself floating in and out of weary midparalysis, and all I could see was the dark sky and the flutter of my own eyelids, a fleshy curtain slipping down; I had half-seen dreams of my husband and the seagull, their souls shifting in and out of each other's body— sometimes my husband was inside a seagull and sometimes a seagull was inside my husband—and this went on for a while until I reached some kind of legal limit for this kind of thing, according to the man who woke me up, a morning sky behind him, this man who seemed smaller than my backpack—he was saying, *Good morning, good morning, good morning*, as loud as it seemed he could, so I woke up looking at this stranger wishing me a good morning, but I knew he didn't want me to have a particularly good morning—he wanted me to collect myself, get myself together, show him my passport, stand up, yes, stand up now, thank you.

Have you been taking drugs? You been out on the piss?

Nope. No drugs, I said.

Then have you been on the piss—have you been drinking heavily?

Not even lightly.

You came here by yourself?

(And when the cop said *by yourself*, I remembered

that day many months before when I got on a bus in Brooklyn heading to a city beach alone on a grey Tuesday, and when I asked the bus driver if this bus was going to the beach he had said, *You're going to the beach by yourself?*, and he said it in a laughing, disbelieving voice and I felt small and silly and lost, though I wasn't lost—I was just in Brooklyn on my way to Queens, a surmountable distance from my apartment and everything in it. *You want to go to the beach? The beach?* the bus driver asked. *Today? By yourself?* And I said, *Yeah*, and he said, *Why you going to the beach all on your own? What you can do on a beach by yourself?* And I said something, explained myself. *This lady's going to the beach by herself,* he said to a woman getting on the bus, but she didn't say anything, just dropped her money into the thing that eats it.)

But this little policeman was less amused by my by-myself-ness and he just asked for my passport and he looked at it and me and said I shouldn't sleep in public—it's just not safe—and I thought he was deeply concerned, that he cared deeply and loved all of humanity, this cop, but that probably wasn't true and I wondered why some people combinations create inaudible noises and others don't and the cop walked away like I was nothing, nothing at all, just some harmless, lost small animal with a passport.

26

I found a pay phone and called the number and I expected it just to ring and ring like last time, to realize
that I might never find Jaye again, or that she might
have given me a fake number, or that I'd have to find
some other way to get back to that inaudible noise,
which I could no longer generate just by thinking of
Jaye, but then Jaye's voice smashed through, and she
said I'd called just in time, and where was I, and she
told me to stay right there, so I did. She drove up in a
tiny silver car with the roof folded back and her hair
tied up in a yellow scarf, and I thought, for a moment,
I'd be just fine forever.

She drove fast along a road that curved with the
ocean and she spoke words I couldn't hear over the
engine whirring and the ocean groaning, and I wanted
to tell Jaye about the inaudible noise but there was no
good way to explain it without shedding too much
light on the inaudible noise, overexposing it, bleach-
ing it white and lifeless, so I closed my eyes and leaned
back and the salty air filled up my head and covered
my face like the gentle hands of every person in the
world who was in love with anyone, and I felt my

joints loosen and the strain of my beach sleep melt away.

We're going back to Wellywood, she said, because she'd changed her mind about spending New Year's with her ballistic family—*and can you believe my mother still calls me Jared? Who's Jared? I don't know any fucking Jared*, Jaye said, and I didn't know any fucking Jared either and I understood she didn't want to think of the way the past was packed into that name, the he she'd been born in—and I could not blame her and I did not blame her and I understood, somehow, something I knew I couldn't really understand. Jaye put on music and belted along to it and I sat silent and still.

I wish I could understand what happened the few days we spent at her apartment in Wellington, but the short of it is that the inaudible noise was slowly overtaken by the minor chord so I avoided Jaye so I could avoid the minor chord and I spent long days out wandering the city, sneaking in late, sneaking out early, and on New Year's Eve I lied and said I felt sick so I needed to stay in—but the next day she caught me coming home in the afternoon—*Happy New Year, love! So you're feeling better then? Got a little fresh air, did ya?*— and I knew I wasn't her love and nothing was new about this year because it had shown up just like all the rest of them and there was something sick and strange about how she was acting as if everything was fine and maybe to her it was, because maybe she'd never heard the inaudible noise and didn't miss it like I did and didn't notice the minor chord—she told me

she had a surprise outing planned for us and it was
time to go and I dreaded what it would be, how she
might surprise me. The minor chord was playing softly
but increasingly unsoftly in the background as we took
a bus and walked through the concrete part of the
city and we ended up on an outdoor basketball court
where a small crowd had gathered and some women
and men made excited noises at Jaye and threw arms
around her and my name was said and repeated at
me—*This is Elyria*—*This is Elyria*—*And this is Elyria*—
and I wanted to be anyone else but I wasn't anyone
else and then it was *time*, someone said, and everyone
sat down on the concrete court and four people
dressed like vintage clowns came in, two in a shopping cart, one pushing the shopping cart, one sort of
rolling across the ground and they began a sort of
presentation of themselves, a routine that hinged on
the humor of how sometimes some people do things
incorrectly, and Jaye was laughing her hearty laugh
and I didn't understand why everyone was laughing
as if they'd never be dead and I wondered why no one
else could hear the harshness and hugeness of the
minor chord and I tried to put myself elsewhere, to
slip into a kind of open-eyed sleep, and I may have
accomplished that because I have no memory of how
the rest of the clown show went, just that the ending
involved a pot of some kind of gruel, some kind of
oatmeal goop, and the climax of this entire show involved the clowns serving us bowls of this gruel, their
eyes all huge, their mouths hanging open in awe of
themselves, and one of them tried to hand me a bowl

of this goop and I didn't want it, and Jaye was looking at me and the clown was looking at me and the clown took my hand and put it around the bowl and put a spoon in the other hand and mimed eating as if to say that was what I should do and I didn't want to do that but Jaye was eating her goop and laughing and saying, *Oh, eat it, love, it's just terrible, so terrible it's great*, and no accidental missile was hitting the city and putting an end to this, so I put the goop bowl on the court and got up and left and Jaye said, *Love? Love?* She said *love* like a question and I said, *I'm not feeling so well*, and she said, *Oh, love*, she said *love* like the name of a dog that had just done something bad, and when Jaye got home she didn't ask me if I was okay because I was locked in the guest room and I woke up early and left with my pack on before she woke up. I did this because I knew the inaudible noise was gone and I knew I wasn't part of the kind of people that can eat a clown's gruel and the wildebeest was throwing its weight around in me and I was trying not to get too beat up by the wildebeest.

Eventually it was night and I walked and I ended up in a pub, and the room, I realized, was crowded with people who all seemed to know and love each other and they also knew that they didn't know or love me and probably never would. I looked at my feet and noticed how the months-long heat of moving had melted the soles down, and I knew that the disrepair of my shoes gave something away about me—but I was always doing this, wearing shoes until they had been burned down to barely anything and I remembered that day at my mother's house years ago when

she had tried to get me to take an old pair of Ruby's
sneakers, a pair of light blue ones that she didn't think
Ruby had ever worn—*They're still in the box*—and I
hadn't understood then that all she was offering me
was a pair of shoes because my shoes were barely the
approximation of shoes, just these worn-out, five-year-
old Sambas that I'd kept not throwing out though
they clearly needed to be thrown out—but that afternoon I'd said, *No, no thanks, I'm okay,* because I wasn't
okay about borrowing shoes I could never return to
Ruby and I couldn't put my feet where her feet should
be and also I was nauseous over the fact that I had
even been given that option, of putting my feet where
the feet of my mother's dead daughter should be, because I knew that I was her other dead daughter, just
not her favorite dead daughter—*They'll just go to waste,*
she said, and *How does your husband let you leave the
house like that? What other option do you have?*—but I
took the other option (*You have two options,* he had
said, *two options*) and the option I took was living with
what I had, which, sure, wasn't an indication that I
could take care of myself, and these heavily damaged
and barely useful shoes made it clear that I needed
help, that my feet were in need, that I needed a better
shoe option, that I needed a better option, that I needed
to get it together, to get a life together, to get myself
together, to get myself. I hadn't gotten myself in a while
and I maybe wasn't going to get myself, it seemed, because my self had been, somehow, ungotten or forgotten or not getting it, whatever it was, or is, or had been,
or would be that I didn't get.

As I sat at the bar and I began to have the feeling I

was a tin of dog food errantly placed on the exotic-fruit aisle with the tinned lychees and pineapple tid-bits and I also knew that I was not a tin of dog food because a tin of dog food would have the luxury to simply be its dense and nothing self, and a tin of dog food wouldn't push and wish against its tinned-ness, wouldn't need to get anything.

Two women came up and put a plastic crown on the head of an oval-faced man standing near me at the bar. It was his birthday, it seemed, because the little crown had *Happy Birthday* written in purple cursive on it and even though every person who could read the crown was probably not the one having the birth-day, something was still understood. What I was to do with my hands suddenly became a distinct and un-solvable problem and I shifted slightly down the bar, toward a wall, to make room for all the people who cared that the oval-headed man had been born, then sitting at the bar seemed like a sad, pathetic place to sit. I couldn't remember why coming to a bar was the choice that I had made, a clearly foolish, desperate, sad-looking choice, and I accidentally made eye con-tact with a man hunched over his arms on the other end of the bar and his eyes said something to me, asked me something people are always silently asking in these kinds of places and I wanted to scream at him, *Don't bother*, but I just tilted my head to the wall and mouthed those words to myself, hoping he'd some-how get the signal.

27

Cars went, but I wasn't sure if it was safe for me to be sharing time and space with other people, who all seemed so much gentler and safer and less of a secret to themselves than I felt I was, so I stood a considerable distance from the highway, backpack still on, a little shrub at my feet, and it seemed the shrub, too, had slept in a stranger's backyard last night, and we stood by the highway both looking as if we'd been left here by accident, as if we were waiting for someone to remember us and come back and take us home, and I noticed the elaborate story I'd made for this little plant and wondered if I was just projecting a story of myself onto him, but the shrub and I just stood there, vague and waiting, until a car came and took me some miles from where I'd been and I stood, again, alone, listening to the ocean falling over itself, hitting rocks, and I thought about going to the beach to have an idealistic moment with the ocean, but all the romance of travel had shriveled and now the ocean wasn't such a thing to me; I was just trying to get somewhere, and later some bloke dropped me off in a little town, by a park that was in a neighborhood where people who don't go to parks live, a neighborhood where people who do go to parks wouldn't want to go. There was a monument by the entrance with some benches surrounding it. After a while two people walked up and sat on the ledge of the monument. They were dressed in identical outfits—school uniforms—white polo shirts and navy pants. They began kissing. One person was a boy with shaggy blond hair and the other was a girl with short black hair. They kissed rhythmically, their mouths the only point of contact, and I ignored them, or not quite ignored them but started reading a book, and while I looked at the book I started thinking of when I wore school uniforms and went with my boyfriend to a park to kiss in the spot where we thought no one would notice, except for that one woman who noticed that one time as she was passing in her hot-pink jogging outfit, the woman who said, *Ah, young love!*, in a tone that was not entirely unkind, and I thought it wasn't kind to make us conscious of our youth and our then-uncomplicated love. I stared at my book, moving my eyes across the letters and thinking of that woman, of *Ah, young love!* and of her hot-pink jogging suit and of the wet smirk on that boyfriend's face as she speed-walked away. The two uniformed people were still kissing, diligently nodding their faces together at a steady tempo.

I stayed in that park until the sun went down and then I stayed longer. I found a bench not near a street-light and did something like sleep for some hours. In the middle of the night I found a jar in a trash bin and I pissed in it and then I placed the jar back in the

trash bin and I know that may seem a little ridiculous, but I thought it gave sleeping in a park just a
shred of dignity if I didn't pee right into the dirt like
an animal, that if I could contain my own waste then
I was somehow a person on an adventure, not a person with limited options and limited means and possibly dwindling sanity.

In the morning, there were birds. There were birds
here just like there are birds anywhere.

28

Sometimes, I realized, many emotions sit on a face, at odds: a lip curl, a neck tilt, an echo in an eye. This was clear when the shed door opened and a woman was there and she didn't seem too surprised by me being there, slumped sideways and using a wad of garden gloves as a pillow and I squinted from the sudden light and she said, *Oh, dear*, and she seemed happy and annoyed at the same time, pinched brow, tiny smile, her eyes doing something else entirely.

Well, good morning, she said, and I said something and she said, *Is everything all right?*

(And everything was not all right because I had been wandering for days or weeks, unsure of where I was going, eating from trash bins, being *alone*, the way Werner said I wasn't meant to be, and I would show him, I thought, except I'd show him without actually showing him, because he wouldn't see me sleeping in sheds and under grapevines in pitch-black vineyards because I'd done that all alone, waiting for daylight, waiting for an idea of what to do with myself, wondering if this kind of aloneness was what I really wanted—)

I'm all right, I said, but she didn't say anything else and I realized she was waiting on more of an explanation, but all my explanations seemed to be at odds with my mouth, were on strike, had called in sick, or maybe never existed and I felt like crucial organs had taken off in the middle of the night, like my kidneys had crawled up my body and out my ears and left two small sandbags in their place and all my lymph nodes had been burned into charcoal lumps—

I was walking and got lost, I finally said. *It was dark. I'm sorry.*

No reason to apologize, dear, it happens to the best of us.

It does not, I thought but did not say, because I knew I was not a part of *the best of us*, and these kinds of things did not happen to *the best of us*, just to *some of us* in extremely rare cases when a person forgets how to reach any reasonable wing of herself, but I wasn't going to go correcting this woman (*Ruth*, she said, putting her hand out to help me up) because I knew, at least, that telling a stranger that you couldn't reach any reasonable wing of yourself just wasn't a pleasant or helpful thing to say, not a good first impression, not a thing to say in daylight.

Ruth sighed and smiled. *Stay for brekkie, then? Get cleaned up?*

The house was antique and silent, and she showed me to a little, white bathroom and said I could use the green soap, the one shaped like a seashell. I unlatched my backpack and let it thud behind me and shed all my clothes and turned on the claw-foot tub, and I stared into a mirror, my tanned skin exaggerating the white in my eyes, hair wisps curling with sweat, dirt smeared around my face.

When the tub filled I slid in and soaked and forgot where I was and I thought about the question of whether the police had taken away the papers that Ruby had dropped off at the professor's office that day, because once I had asked him if he still had those papers and he said he wasn't sure where they had gone; and I said, *You don't remember? Why don't you remember?* Husband: *It was a long time ago, Elly, and it was a very difficult year—* And I: *But why wouldn't you remember what happened to them?* And he'd said nothing or something that amounted to nothing, and I tongued this memory like a burn in my mouth until the bathwater cooled and shook me back into my body where my fingerprints were ruffled.

In the living room an elderly woman was slumped like a sandbag in an ornate wingback chair.

Nina, I'd like you to meet Elyria, Ruth said. *Elyria, this is Nina.*

Nice to meet you, I said, trying to seem calm and normal and nice—not a woman with a wildebeest renting a room in her, not a woman who sleeps in garden sheds and phone booths and anywhere—but my voice sounded like I had borrowed it and it didn't fit my mouth, not my real thoughts made into real words, but some awkward hand-me-down.

It's lovely to meet you, dear, Nina said, not looking up. Her belly paunch looked like risen dough.

Mother, Ruth said, *you could make an effort at the very least.*

A what?

An effort, Ruth said louder, *you could—would you just sit up? We have a guest, Mother, really.*

Fine, fine, Nina said, but she didn't move any part of herself. She was wearing five or six pearl necklaces tangled together. A bowl of wet blueberries was balanced on her gut and a tear of blueberry skin was wedged between her front teeth.

I'm just going to the garden for some herbs, Ruth said. *I'll be right back. There's coffee and tea if you'd like it.*

Nina looked around the room as if someone might try to sneak up on her, then looked at me.

So, how is it? Sleeping in the garden shed?

Oh, it's just okay, I said.

I think it sounds like fun. I'd like to have some fun again. Once I slept sitting up on a train. Imagine that. A young woman all dressed to travel—just sleeping—sitting up sleeping with her gloves and hat still on!

After I went at a plate of scrambled eggs and toast like a stray dog, then a second plate, then a bowl of fruit and more butter-heaped toast, Ruth started asking questions (the expected ones: where-was-I-from, where-was-I-going, why-had-I-slept-in-her-shed) and I tried to sip tea as if I was the kind of person who sipped tea as I told her the truth: that I wasn't lost because I no longer had a destination, that the place I'd wanted to stay in New Zealand had fallen through and the backup plan had fallen through. *I really do enjoy being alone*, I told her, and I tried to smile, but I realized that I wasn't quite smiling and what was happening was there was water on my face and it was coming from my eyes and this was surprising to me, but it didn't seem to surprise Ruth, who tilted her head and asked about my family as if she was a therapist, someone accustomed to sudden, naked pain, and I found myself unable to lie like I had so many other times.

I told her about my husband and Ruby and my mother and I told her everything and I was so tired by the end of it and my chest was shaking and I exhaled and I felt a little relaxed and Ruth, with her concerned and respectably wrinkled face and her silk blouse and pale lilac trousers and the scent of rosemary haloing this emphatically wholesome situation called her life, Ruth looked at me and said, *Would you like to call someone, dear?* And all I could do was agree with her because it would have been nearly impossible or possibly illegal or at the least difficult to disagree with her wholesomeness— I said, *Okay*, and she brought a rotary phone out and the only number that came to mind was the number my mother would write in Magic Marker along my forearm when she sent Ruby and me out to play—*Just in case, you can never be too careful*—and sometimes you couldn't tell her fours and nines apart—*Thatsanine, notta four*—and Ruby and I would mimic her later, *Thatsanine, thatsanine,* we'd say this invented word to other kids who had no idea and we'd smirk at each other and run through sprinklers to wash off the Magic Markered number, and we'd say, *We're never going back now, she'll never find us now*, but we always went back and we always remembered the number and I don't know why I dialed that number that afternoon at Ruth's house, but I dialed it as if I had finally found the case she'd meant by *just in case*, and just like that there was a skeptical *Hello* on the line and I said, *It's Elyria.*

Oh . . . , my mother said. *Elyria? Huh.*

I'm okay, I said.

I thought you might be, she said, *you always seem to manage. Where is it you went?*

New Zealand.

Well, that's pretty far.

We were quiet for a moment and she said, *Are you still there?*

Yes.

You know, there was a moment there we all thought you were dead. Is that what you wanted us to think?

I realized it was early evening there, so she'd maybe only had a few afternoon vodkas. I told her that I didn't want anyone to think I was dead, that I just wanted to leave.

You know, Elly, I really thought you'd be over all this by now. It's been six years.

I stared at Ruth's whitewashed china cabinet.

Hello? Are you there?

I'm here, I said.

Well, don't you have anything to say about that, Elyria? Anything?

About what?

You leave on the anniversary of—you know . . . It's always been about Ruby for you, even the marriage—you

know that—everyone knows that. I'm just the only one that
will say it.

She laughed a little and audibly sipped something.

That's not what it's about. I didn't—I didn't even know
it was . . . But I must have known it was, I realized,
somehow, I must have known. I let the silence settle.

Are you there? . . . Elyria?

I'm here, I said, but I knew, increasingly, I wasn't
here, and I felt that able-to-weep-and-be-seen version
of myself that I'd been with Ruth hardening again,
like warm caramel left to cool.

For the record, I told him not *to cancel your cards, that*
was his idea, Elyria, because he didn't care if you were safe,
he just cared if you were his. *Do you see how twisted he is*
now? Marrying his dead student's sister? A decade between
the two of you? That never struck you as strange?

But my mother didn't know what it was like to be
in the diner with the sudden sense that was made between that professor and me, when we were not yet a
husband and a wife, but a young woman and a young
professor, people who suddenly had something that
the other needed, a possibility, a particular balm, and
I still don't know how to adequately describe it or understand it, but it made everything make sense, made
getting married make sense, made the guaranteed and
steady supply of loss in every life make sense, and
then it all changed, somehow, or killed itself, or wandered out and never came back, and that was why I
had left, not Ruby, not the lack of Ruby—

I think I need to go, I said, because I was done being
reminded of the difference between us, and I hung up

the phone and Ruth came back into the room and asked me if I felt better and I said I did feel better because I had turned back into the woman who could fold herself up like an acrobat and store herself away, packed like a body bent inside a cannon, and my face went back to its cool, normal state, not its warm, wet, and helpless animal state and she said, *You look better, dear, maybe that's all you needed, just to talk to your mother for a moment*, and I said, *Yes, thank you. That was all I needed.*

29

When the black truck slowed and stopped I realized this truck had slowed and stopped for me before— there was that empty-nested woman, that little bird for herself.

I got in and she said, *And where are we headed today, mademoiselle?* And she smiled. I felt guilty that she was smiling because I knew I was going to tell her that I had lied, there was no farmer husband and I was going nowhere, over and over, always going nowhere.

I don't mind going . . . anywhere, I guess.

Well, she said, and I braced for it, the question that was going to lead to an answer that would lead to a confession that wasn't nice and wasn't comfortable—

What does your husband think of you going just anywhere by yourself?

I lied, I said, *I didn't come here with my husband. He doesn't even know where I am*, and once I said all that I felt myself lighten but the atmosphere in the truck darkened because it's disappointing enough to know that the people we love will sometimes lie but it is almost worse when we remember that strangers do this,

too, and this is why it is best not to admit our lies to
strangers, because it is not pleasant to learn that someone will lie even when there is little to nothing at stake,
and it's not pleasant to remember that we have all believed other strangers' lies, and even though almost
every living person knows this, in a way, it's still not
the best thing to bring up in polite conversation. If the
widow had asked, I would have told her the rest of
the story, the grey meat of it, but she didn't ask. She
put the truck in drive and drove and she didn't ask
me why I'd gone through all this trouble. Probably a
more powerful part of herself was telling some less
powerful part to just *leave it—leave it—*the way I've
heard people tell their dogs to stop being interested
in stinking gristle on a hot sidewalk.

She let me out at a visitors' center in a town that
seemed close to nothing, just cliff faces and bridges
over narrow rivers. *Someone can help you in there, tell
you where you should go,* and I was thankful that she
was right—inside there was a wall tacked with flyers,
one said *Bakers Needed,* and another said *Farmhands
Needed,* and there were other needs, needs I either
couldn't meet or didn't want to meet, but one just said
Live on Waiheke Island, Live in Paradise! and I liked
that it didn't ask anything of me, just told me what to
do, emphatically. *Lodging and meals for labour, many
skills needed,* so I took the flyer off the board and called
the number and a woman answered—*Do you mind
weeding, housekeeping, laundry, light repairs?*—and even
though I did mind those things I had realized by sleeping in sheds and parks and yards that Werner wasn't

totally wrong and wasn't totally right: I'm not a person who needs people, but I am the kind of person who needs to be near people who don't need me. So I told the woman I didn't mind any of those things and she said I could come whenever, and that's how easy it was to find a makeshift life, a life blind to the past and future.

After being picked up again, then let out in a sulfur-smelling parking lot by a row of train tracks and picked up again and let out at a petrol station and picked up for one last time by a bucktoothed woman driving a pale grey van, I ended up in Auckland, and as I got out of the van the bucktoothed woman said, *God bless you*, which I followed, as if by reflex, with a sneeze, so she said it again—*God bless you*—and I sneezed again, and I thought this was the kind of thing that people make easy, laughing eye contact over, that life is funny sometimes, or maybe not funny but maybe somewhat unexpected, but the bucktoothed woman kept her face as plain as a curtain, her two front teeth bucking right out of her lips like they were the other two in the holy trinity of she.

30

Luna said she was vegetarian for *purely physical reasons* as she slid a wet pile of diced onion off the side of a knife and into a hot skillet and she did this with unnerving precision, and the onions hissed, and I imagined Luna pushing a javelin through a white rabbit for fun because she said she knew she could easily kill an animal—killing wasn't the problem—but she didn't want to ingest dead flesh, to absorb a death, and the skewered-rabbit-on-javelin image, combined with her knife skills and the way she was looking at me, made me wonder what her body could do to a thing if it wanted to do anything to another thing, and this memory has always come to me link-armed with another memory of a morning when Luna was just eating a piece of fruit—maybe an apple but an apple has obvious implications, allegorical and otherwise, and maybe a peach, but a peach has other implications, sexual and otherwise, and I know I don't entirely remember what kind of fruit it was, and I am not even certain that this moment ever happened in real life, but I do have a feeling that I once saw the lush flare of her lips as she bit into something and a certain purse as she chewed.

This was during the first week of the many months I lived in a caravan behind Luna and Amos's cabin, back when I still thought I had solved the problem of who I was, of why I couldn't seem to go about life the way other people did—I was beginning to realize that what I wanted was the noise of people living near me, but not near enough to cause any inaudible noises to show up because I knew that those sorts of noises often shift into inaudible minor chords and I am unable to deal with that shift—when love or kindness or inaudible noises turn into boredom or disappointment or minor chords—and this is the difference between me and the rest of the world: most people can let their feelings shift without a wildebeest smashing them up from the inside, but I, for some reason, cannot—and, still, I am more human than wildebeest so I'll never be exempt from the human need for other people to be near, but because I am part wildebeest they can't be too near, and I would like to apologize for that but I can't apologize for that, I can't apologize to everyone who deserves an apology for it, unless no one deserves anything, in which case, what a relief, because I can give everyone that nothing—I can give them nothing all day.

But this theory hadn't completely set during those early days with Luna and Amos and their extremely organic and well-ordered life, their highly organized toolshed and their biodynamic kiwi orchard where the hens roamed around laying eggs without regret or reserve, and I noticed that Luna and Amos smiled shamelessly and openly at each other and aside from the fact that Luna knew she was an animal capable of killing other animals, neither of them seemed to have a dark corner of themselves and why is it that some people turn out like that—Luna and her constant smiling and her glowing skin and her hair shining and thick, and she was young, maybe even younger than me, and I knew she was one of these women whose youth would stick around longer than average and even though Amos was in the part of his life where his wrinkles were not just visible, but obvious, he still usually had this calm expression on his face, as if to say, yes, his life had mostly already happened, but he had won and would continue to win and here he was with his well-worked hands and heavily sunned skin and hand-hewn cabin and his pretty little wife, and all their unashamed smiles. Some people just turn out like that and other people live in caravans behind those people's cabins, trading chores for a place to sleep.

If Luna could tell that I was a person who wasn't entirely all right, she must have overlooked that, or maybe was just profoundly bored and lonely in her well-ordered, organic, seaside, photo-ready life because in those first weeks she was always trying to create some kind of understanding between us, which reminded me that it is hard for me to understand people who want to understand me and be understood; Luna (she must have been flatly unaware) was always inviting me to make dinner with her and she was trying to ask me about what my life consisted of, was there a love in my life, what had I done before New Zealand, what did I hope to do next, and I tried to be good, I tried to be a good woman with good answers to these questions and I tried to appreciate how Luna wanted to share a bottle of wine with me and explain to me why it was special and I wanted to appreciate the stories she told me about how she had met Amos and how it was a whirlwind romance but I found, increasingly, that I did not particularly care and I tried to fake a little kindness, a little sweetness, tried to mirror Luna back at herself, but that exhausted me after a week and I concluded that I was not meant for this sort of thing, friends, friendliness, no, I wasn't meant for it. I was meant to earn my keep and just keep my keep, that's all.

A week or so later, a group of people showed up and they all wore similar linen tunics and much of their hair was growing in wads. They put their hands together and bowed a good deal. None of them seemed to own or wear shoes. I almost wanted to know more about them, how they all met, why they seemed to have a uniform, what they had against shoes, but the desire to know more was overridden by the knowledge that to get that information I would have to actually speak with them a substantial amount and that they might have questions about me and that it might be difficult to extract myself from such a situation.

I was making dinner for the group one night (I had been demoted to the most domestic jobs, which I always did alone) when Amos came in to wash his hands.

Your family must be—

No family. I don't have a family.

Amos nodded. I knew there must have been a point in his life when he would have said the same thing, that he had no family, even though I knew Amos had probably made this new family with Luna to overshadow the one he had come from and knowing how to lie in the same way gave us a common truth. There was a pause here of about three seconds, then Amos turned on the faucet to wash his hands. There was another pause of about four seconds, then I went back to chopping carrots.

You're chopping too quickly, he said, *no reason to rush the knife.*

The knife is fine.

Aye, the knife is fine, it's your hands that need the minding.

The what?

The minding.

There was a pause of maybe one second. Amos started to reexplain, but I cut him off.

Oh, the minding. To mind my hands. Okay.

This kept happening, this thing where I didn't know what a person speaking in English was saying. It felt rude to keep asking what someone said only to figure it out and repeat the word back in my accent but I didn't know another way to deal with this problem, so this was how I dealt with it.

Sorry, I said.

Amos left to deal with one of the animals so I finished chopping the carrots without any damage to any part of my hand or self, then I chopped the broccoli and peppers and potatoes and put oil and salt on the chopped vegetables and put them in the oven and waited awhile, then took them out, but the problem with this was I wasn't minding the oven like Amos had said I should do—*Mind the oven*, he said, *it's shit*—and I agreed now, it was shit, because it had blackened one corner of the pan of vegetables; but I had been thinking about my husband and how we would likely, very likely, almost certainly, practically absolutely, not see each other for a long time or ever and even if we did it would never be the same and so, in this way, we were both dead to each other, alive only in shape-shifting memory, but dead in every other way. And because I was still thinking about my half-dead husband as I took the half-burned vegetables out of the oven, I just scraped them all into a big bowl instead of taking the burned ones out first because I was trying to count how many days it had been since my husband and I had died to each other instead of looking at the charcoaled broccoli and carrots and realizing they weren't the kind of thing that people liked to eat. I tried to pick the burned ones from the bowl but I didn't get many of them because I didn't make much of an effort, and even though I was taking the burned ones out because they weren't edible, I ate them because, at the moment, I thought it would be better if everyone learned to consume their own mistakes.

31

I want to watch that video you showed me once of the twin babies saying the same syllable to each other over and over and over. I want to watch that because we both know that's all life is, really, that's all it is. We're all twins and clones and remakes of each other; we're all pairs unpaired; we're all speaking the same repeated syllable at each other and why is it that I have to go running off into a twinless solitude? What is inside this solitude but me, saying the same syllable to myself over and over and over, trying to make sense of it, trying to rearrange it. Husband, if I was actually speaking to you I'd tell you about the baby Grand Emperor penguin who swam two thousand miles accidentally and ended up on a beach near Wellington, a long accident, a wrong turn. They said he ate sand and driftwood, for lack of knowing what to eat, where he was, what he needed, why he'd swum two thousand miles away from the other penguins, but I'm still wondering about the months he spent swimming alone. Maybe sharks swam past him. Maybe schools of tiny white fish nipped at his feet, grew disinterested, swam on. Maybe grey whales rose beneath his tininess, a single bulging whale eye as large as his head as he swam through the blue daytime ocean and the navy storming ocean and the cold black ocean under a moon or a half-moon or no moon at all, and each night above him a different moon was there, and the moon's slow wink was all for him, for his solitude, for his perseverance, for the constant plane of water, water, water, and no one who loved him and nothing he knew and no others to swim with at all. What was he but a pair unpaired, living away from the other penguins' cold huddle? Enough with my ridiculous metaphor. Maybe it is time for me to be clear, or let me be clearer than I have yet been: I didn't leave you to become someone else's something, someone else's twin to talk to, someone else's clone to mirror, someone else's anything. It was not that kind of leaving. I am not that kind of gone. I am gone but not so gone that there is no possibility of me coming back, though maybe I have gone out far enough now that you are preparing for a future without this particular wife—so, Husband, if this is so, please keep in mind you are still legally obligated to me, written like a law into my life, and we cannot remove ourselves from each other so easily, with such impulse, or, at least, this is somewhat true. I, you should know, left without a particular reason, though I may have a few nonparticular reasons— unnamable feelings and unnamable secrets and un-understandable feelings, feelings about secrets and feelings about facts and feelings about feelings, and since they are all un-understandable can we call them *derstandable* feelings? Why was it that we grew to *derstand* each other? Where did that *derstanding* come from and why couldn't we pry ourselves away from it and why were we never together anymore, just alone in each other's vicinity? And is there any possibility that we could become, again, the kind of people who have a future instead of just a past and could we reach some kind of clearing in that future, some grassy patch of many-years-from-now where we are just fine being just fine? Maybe we could decide to get a dog or a child or just a good bottle of wine and maybe we'll sit at a sidewalk café, sipping it, sipping our lack of responsibilities, watching mothers bumble by lugging their children and babies and unhelpful dogs, all the weight and moan of their decisions hanging on them and asking, always asking for more, to be fed, to be watched, to be loved, and if we must be either children people or dog people, I will say that it makes me feel the least unwell to believe that we could become dog people, not children people, in that distant patch of grassy future. Because I believe we can follow the simple repeated emotion of a dog, the predictable needs of a dog, the gentle forgetfulness of a dog—and you may have wanted children in the past and I may have wanted to want children in the past and maybe you only wanted to want but disguised that wanting to want as simple wanting, and perhaps I just wanted children but couldn't manage to admit it as anything other than a wanting of a want because I feared the burden of a plain want, the frightening possibility of a desire, of a desire that would not necessarily be met or the possibility of that desire being met unpeacefully—but no matter now, that was some fork in the hypothetical road we didn't take and now we can stay here in this unwanting, this past-our-timeness, this future and its disintegrating idea of the past. I am still sometimes hopeful that I could someday try to generate a desire to raise a dog, to meet the repeated needs of a dog, the simple dogness of dogs, all the qualities of dogs that they do not share with babies, those pre-people people and all their warm, slimy wanting and their embarrassingly exaggerated needs, their screaming red-faced hunger and their bloody-murder nap-needing, and how those needs are just the same as ours, only magnified and reflected back at us—and do you know what? Some people are not the kind of people who can stand those kinds of things, magnified and reflected things, warm, slimy, needing tiny-people things. Some people just prefer dogs. Husband, I know as well as you that all my metaphors have turned bizarre, but what I need to say is there is a future and I am in it. There may be a tomorrow when I might come home and maybe it won't be too late for me to become the kind of woman who doesn't feel her life is irrevocably complicated, and maybe I can slowly forget what happened to my brain, where it went and why I couldn't find it and why you couldn't find it either. But if I never come home, Husband, please know I still have many of the same senses of belonging to you. I still have a little ring around my brain like a diamond one or a Saturn one or the kind that bathwater leaves. I am asking you, I know, to suffer, to stand very still and feel as little as possible.

32

Even though the air was cooling daily and the sun was setting earlier than it once had, the linen-tunic people still went without shoes and still slept in a thin-walled yurt, and I imagined they slept in a pile the way that puppies or kittens sleep, but I slept in the metal caravan the way a sardine would if sardines came canned individually. It was apparent that a unity had happened between the linen tunics and Amos and Luna, and I was not a part of that unity, that community of people all enjoying, respecting, supporting each other. They would linger over dinner at night, eat lunch together outside instead of swallowing aspirin washed down with goat's milk like I did. I'd been given, or volunteered for, or just always *did* the jobs that I could do alone—searching out the eggs in the kiwi orchard, making dinner for everyone while they built that barn together, holding the ladder steady while another climbed, while they chanted *one-two-three-and-go* before raising the barn's frame or things like that. And though I had noticed that I was separate from this pseudofamily I did not see a problem with it and I thought no one else saw a problem with

it and I thought that probably meant that there was
no problem with it, but that all changed one afternoon
when Amos asked if he could speak to me for a minute and he didn't wait for me to answer him and he
didn't speak for just a minute, he spoke for several of
them and he spoke like fathers in television shows
speak when they have something simple that they want
to explain in a complicated way in order to seem enig-
matic, maybe, in order to seem to be the keeper of
some sort of wisdom only bestowed upon a man of
a certain age and he told me something about biody-
namics or permaculture or something, how the system
relies on a total cooperation or integration or some
other gration.

*You know, we're trying to create a full community
here—this is important to us. And we can respect your pri-
vacy, you know, I get that, but we really do need you to par-
ticipate in our ecosystem, Elyria. Can you do that?*

And I didn't say anything for a moment and Amos
was doing this look my husband used to do sometimes,
this look that was a cross between pity and doing
long division in his head, so I mirrored that long-
division-pity back at him and Amos finally said, *Do
you think you could be a part of our ecosystem?* And the
voice of a teenage girl came up in me, silently, and
asked, *How am I supposed to know?* and it was the voice
of that girl in the episode of the soap opera when she
gets arrested and the cop asks her, *What's a girl like you
doing getting arrested?*, and she says, *How am I supposed
to know?* in the same annoyed, indignant way I'd just
heard it in my head and I realized that those must have

NOBODY IS EVER MISSING

been what my feelings were—annoyed, indignant—
and I couldn't feel them, but I could hear them, so
maybe I was something like that boy I'd gone to high
school with who had been born without fully functioning nerves, who had fingers and hands covered in
cuts and burns because he loved to cook but didn't
really understand a knife or a flame, that boy who all
the other boys teased because he couldn't have a real
penis if he didn't have the feelings that came with it, so
he wasn't a man because he didn't know the difference
between pain and pleasure, and that boy never seemed
to smile and he wore long sleeves year-round, and I was
not so different from him—we were both unable to get
near the real life in life.

I believe I could do that, I said to Amos and he smiled,
so I smiled a little and I was glad I had pretended to
be better than I was because it would make it easier to
leave because I knew I couldn't live up to this pretend
person I had made up and presented to Amos and it
was nearly autumn now so maybe something needed
to die, something needed to change, and at the same
time I knew I didn't know what would happen next,
what would die or change, and I understood that I
had little to no control over what would die or change
next but I had a kind of calmness that was actually
just exhaustion and I also had the house to myself for
a least an hour since Amos had to go teach that permaculture workshop and Luna had taken the arthritic
dog to the vet and what I wanted, impossibly, was for
the professor to be there with me in this house, and I
wanted him to be there because that early version of

the man who became my husband wouldn't say anything to me about how long it had been since we had
died to each other and he wouldn't say anything
about how unfairly I had disappeared and he wouldn't
tell me that I always have two options—*You can choose
how you feel or you can let your feelings choose you*—because
maybe it is true that those were the options that my
husband had, but I knew I didn't have those options
and I hated for someone to tell me that I had options
I didn't have because I knew that my mind was a small
object for sale and my feelings could pick me up and
own me and maybe my husband was too expensive
for feelings to choose him, to pick him up and have
him rung up and scanned and bagged and taken along
with those feelings, feelings of *I can't really get out of
bed today* and *Husband, would you please not talk to me
for the rest of the year.* I, too often, had my face smashed
against concrete curbs of Ruby, memories of Ruby, the
way her face had looked that afternoon as she curled
in that chair by the window and the light streaming
in and the dark streaming out and what happened so
soon after—I went around hostage to those memories,
an invisible person following me with a gun barrel to
my back.

I stepped lightly into Amos's office where he had
an off-limits computer and I went to the university's
website and I went to the mathematics department
page and I tried to load one of my husband's lectures.
I had never watched them because there had never
been a reason to watch them back when my husband
was sitting so calmly in my real life, when we inhab-

ited each other's space like we were long-owned pieces
of clothing, forgotten and familiar on our bodies. I
found a lecture from last April and I opened it, but
only the first image would load, a fuzzy still, a poor
rendering of my memory's memory, but the blur made
him look younger, I realized, and maybe this was what
my husband was like in the decade before we met. His
oldest friends always said he looked the same as he
had at college graduation but I knew his face closely
enough to know that wasn't true—I knew I had
missed so many delicate years of his life and the man
I had married was the hard remainder; I had missed
years of innocent longing and late nights and odd
jobs and girlfriends who were now mothers of someone else's children, I had missed wrinkleless eyes and
his hair before the grey ones crept in and his mouth
before it had said I love you to other people, shadowy
other women I never knew, would never know. All
those selves my husband practiced in the decade before me felt unfair because my past didn't have any of
those secret selves because everyone's childhood and
adolescence are more or less the same, dear struggle,
and my husband had seen me change from an old
child to a young adult and I didn't have a past like he
did—I didn't have a smoother version of me tucked
away in other people's memories.

And after I had deleted my history on Amos's computer I realized that even if no one ever found me,
and even if I lived out the rest of my life here, always
missing, forever a missing person to other people, I
could never be missing to myself, I could never delete

my own history, and I would always know exactly where I was and where I had been and I would never wake up not being who I was and it didn't matter how much or how little I thought I understood the mess of myself, because I would never, no matter what I did, be missing to myself and that was what I had wanted all this time, to go fully missing, but I would never be able to go fully missing—nobody is missing like that, no one has ever had that luxury and no one ever will. It doesn't seem like much now, but realizations rarely do, I suppose, those bright moments when you can finally see something that had been there all along. This wasn't a commodifiable realization, the kind of thing in college essays or inspirational books or the hardbound journals of gentle ladies. There was no *ah*, no *ha*, no relaxation or humor folded into this realization. There was just something real in my head—a rescue boat in a sea where there was no one left to save.

33

While everyone slept I packed and left—down the pebbled path and through the field where the cows all swayed in their standing sleep. I hiked up a path and into the woods, thinking about what I should be thinking about and almost having a real feeling—a feeling like, this is really sad, this is a sad place to be, a sad part of my life, maybe just a sad life. The woods were not particularly beautiful. I was not impressed by the trees.

After I'd been hiking awhile I realized I was no longer hiking, but lying on my back on the side of the trail; I couldn't tell how long I had been there. My body felt like tangled rubber bands and dried-out pens and sticky paper clips, like the contents of a drawer where you put the things you don't have anywhere else to put, and I knew that the mind and body are connected, and that my bodily sensations were just messages from my mind, but I just wished there was a box or a drawer or a hole in the ground where I could put all this, all this mind and body stuff that I didn't know what else to do with. I thought of that woman who worked at a library I had been in at some point,

and how she had these false teeth that had come unstuck in her mouth and were bouncing around in
there as she spoke, and I wondered what that woman
had in her mind that made her fake teeth move like
that, refuse to stay put. Maybe her mind was a puppy.
Maybe her mind was a puppy that had been drinking
soda and chewing on a straw someone had been snort-
ing drugs through and as I realized this I revised my
feelings about the wobble-toothed woman because
even though her dentures had looked as if they might
wobble their way out of her mouth and bite their way
across her face, down her neck to her shoulder, down
her arm, make a leap off her hand, land on me, and
gnaw me into parts—no, I didn't pity her anymore
and I wasn't disturbed anymore and I didn't feel
threatened—I thought, what a lucky woman she is to
have a drugged-up puppy for a mind and I was mo-
mentarily happy for that woman and her irrevocably
wrinkled face and there just was no revoking the time
she'd been through because the things she'd done to
herself and the things that had been done to her would
always be the things she did or had done.

Still on the ground of this trail I wobbled into that
comalike middle ground between waking and sleeping and my thoughts turned off and I said, *Goodbye,
thoughts, goodbye, goodbye.* I was filled with sounds
instead of thoughts, the wind combing through the
tree branches. The crunch and crackle of the deader
parts of the woods. The twitch of the parts that may
have been more alive. And I know now that it still
isn't clear where I am in the spectrum of living and

not living, but I am not and never was the kind of woman who romanticizes natural noises just because they come from nature because tumors and poisons and tornadoes are also natural—not the things you want to romanticize—that's for fiction, the fake, the imaginary—put the romanticizing there, I thought, not on the dirt and fire of life.

Eventually I was hiking again and the trail ended at a paved road and after some time a woman driving a blue van stopped and rolled down her window.

Put it in the back but not on this side, the other side, no, the other side, because he's right there, so go around.

I hadn't even had my thumb out and I didn't know who *he* was or what she meant, but I went to the other side and put my pack in the backseat and it turned out that *he* was a baby, sleeping, strapped into a plastic cradle.

It's very dangerous what you're doing, very stupid. People come here and think this is a country where everyone is nice and good but everyone isn't always nice and good and there are women who get raped and murdered every day, every day, and today might not be the day where everything is so different. So think about that. Think about what you're doing.

I nodded. I said I would think about it, but it was still too early in the day to think about it. She had pretty dark hair. I guessed she was Argentinean.

It just isn't safe to be a woman or girl anywhere anymore. Remember dignities? Well, people misplaced their dignities. Everything is changing. Why is everything changing like that? I don't even know. I just don't know. When I was your age I hitched all over the place, but now—God, I don't know what's happened to people, but they've gone bad, turned sour, all of them.

I said I would be careful and she dropped me off in a big parking lot in Ostend. She said, *Stay away from those bloody blokes.*

I said I would, but I didn't, and a bloke stopped and I got in his bright green camper van.

He said, *Mortis.*

I said, *Mortis?*

He said, *No, Mortis.*

Mortis? I asked again, but he said, *No.*

I said, *I'm Elyria*, then we didn't talk anymore.

Mortis sounded like he was maybe Swiss or something and he drove me to the same place he was going, a small and almost empty beach, without raping or killing me, which I appreciated, and when we got out of his van he said, *Take the care*, and I said, *Take even more*, and pretended like that was the way people spoke in this world because what difference did it make? Who would care if they knew I went around impersonating persons?

I put down my backpack in the sand and noticed a man and a girl in a green swimsuit making a sand castle near the ocean. Farther down the beach there was a woman and past her there was no one and for some reason I thought about the night that I burned those vegetables and how I told Amos and Luna if they got some burned ones on their plates it was all right but they didn't have to eat them, unless they wanted to, because the burned ones do taste okay, but the unburned ones taste better and are also much easier to chew. I walked toward the ocean, my brain somehow calm and empty, sick of itself, taking a sick day.

I waded calf-deep into the water and just looked at the horizon, the ocean curve, and I had an almost ideal moment. I crouched down and put my arms into the water and I felt, actually, peaceful. I huddled against my knees like a child and I closed my eyes awhile and just was.

I started to push myself farther out into the sea, but something fleshy moved over my feet, against my shins and there was a small splash not made by me and I felt a strange electric sensation in my forearm and I raised my arm out of the water and it didn't look right, somehow, but had changed too quickly for me to register what was wrong: there was an addition to my arm, to my forearm, specifically, something poking through the top of it— a dark grey point like the tip of a knife and when I looked at the underside of my arm I saw the rest of it, this metal-looking thing, like a piece of sawing machinery, some kind of hardware, a lost part, but I was in the ocean where hardware pieces are not usually lost and not usually impaling a person's arm.

I was still staring when a rush of blood came out and began dripping into the water and I thought of what that nurse had said so many months ago: that blood is hazardous waste and it must be carefully disposed of and I didn't want my hazardous waste to contribute to the hazardous waste that was already in the ocean so I began walking toward the beach but when

I got to the shore I was bleeding in a way a person might call heavily, and it was only then I felt my head getting light and my limbs going loose in their sockets and I knew I needed to do something about my sudden condition, and, as if I'd figured out a riddle, I realized this hardware had belonged to a stingray, his stinger, and I opened my mouth in that way you do when you figure something out (*Oh, a stingray!*), when chaos turns to order. But the blood was rushing out thicker now and the man who had been building the sand castle with the girl had noticed this hazardous-waste issue I was having and was running toward me and shouting, and it was only then that I felt a tremendous amount of pain, which radiated from that stingray stinger (*What are those things called?*) and at this point I was maybe screaming, jolty and uncontrollable, as if my screams were coming out accidentally, like hiccups. The man picked me up and ran toward the parking lot and I saw Mortis (*Oh, I remember you, Mortis, there you are*) and Mortis had my backpack and was running very calmly, like a good athlete, and in the parking lot I saw the little girl eating an orange Popsicle, and it was melted across her face and arm but when she saw her father she dropped the Popsicle and began shaking her hands and stomping her feet and making a tantrum against this—and who could disagree with her? It is plainly unpleasant to see your father smeared with some stranger's hazardous waste and I remember her whimpering in the backseat as we sped up the road and she kept asking, *Papa, what's going to happen to her? What's going to happen?* And Papa didn't answer for the first few times and I thought, *Good job, Papa, let her keep living in suspense*. But eventually Papa did answer and he said, *I don't know, honey*, and she stopped asking and stopped whimpering or maybe this is when I finally passed out, but before I did I realized I had witnessed the moment when this girl found out that nobody (not even Papa) knows *what's going to happen to her* or him or anyone and that's called Dramatic Tension and that's called the Suspense of Life and that's called Being Alive.

34

I woke up in a small, green room.

A TV was hanging from the ceiling in the corner with a plastic fern hanging under it. I heard a texture of clicks and beeps. One framed picture was on the wall: a man on a sailboat looking at the ocean like it belonged to him, like he'd spent his whole life earning enough money to buy the ocean and now he had it and he was pleased with himself.

In the door there was a small, narrow window for seeing small, narrow things. A woman came in and smiled at me.

Good morning, Elyria. I'm Mrs. Harper. I work for the embassy.

She stared at me and seemed to be waiting on something.

How are you feeling this morning?

A word—I needed a word—*Fine*, I said, a reflex.

The woman showed me some documents, showed me my own passport, and seemed concerned and proud at the same time, like she had just played a hundred-point word in what was supposed to be a friendly game of Scrabble. She read something to me about a law or a bill or an act or an act of God, something—some kind of treatment that had been given or would be given—but all the light and sounds were still blurred. She put a pen in my hand and a clipboard under the pen.

Oh, sorry. Here   you don't usually use that arm, do you?

My right hand and forearm were covered in gauze and once I saw it I felt it, felt my muscles shuddering, felt the bones in my arm humming, the flesh bright and hot. The woman was trying to wrap my stiff left hand around this pen and it felt extremely possible that my whole life had happened and now I was at the end of it, signing something away, my craggle hand and drumless ears and drooping eyes all nearly gone. My signature looked like kindergarten scratch.

She said something about customs and a visa, a penalty, deportation, but I didn't hear the full sentences until she mentioned my husband—

He's being kept up-to-date and has paid for your transportation and medical costs. Due to your history, we have decided to conduct an additional mental health assessment. This is for Homeland Security to use to calculate any risk factors of your repatriation.

I felt myself waking up a little more. Sound started sounding like sound again. I smiled at the painting of the man who had bought the ocean and thought of Mortis. I wondered what happened to Mortis. I enjoyed the word *repatriation*.

Dr. Williamson will be in shortly. Best of luck, she said, but I knew she didn't even wish me the second best or the third or any kind of luck in the top ten of luck or anywhere near it. When she closed the door, I heard the lock click.

35

A nurse came in.

Mrs. Riley, Charles is on the phone.

Charles?

Yes. Charles.

She said this like I should absolutely know who Charles was and I could have no possible excuse for not knowing who Charles was and that even the word *Charles* should have carried a serious meaning to me and I should have already known this meaning and if I did not know what *Charles* meant there was something severely wrong with me.

Your husband, she said. *He's on the phone.*

My husband, I said. His name could have been Charles, I thought, yes, I was mostly sure that *Charles* was the word that people who were not his wife called my husband since they couldn't call him *Husband* because none of them were his wife.

What does Charles say?

He wants to speak with you, she said.

Me?

She just looked this time, saying nothing, like I'd had three shots to get this right and they were up.

Okay, I said. *I'll talk.*

And so I talked.

And also he talked.

And we were talking.

We were having a talk.

We were putting information toward each other and we were doing this as casually as we could pretend to be doing this because it had been a long time since we had done this and we were out of practice and it was obvious to us, obvious that we were unused to each other, but the main problem I had with this talk was that my husband had put his voice on crookedly—he was wearing it incorrectly, was oriented to it in an ugly way and it hurt to listen to him speak like this in the same way that it hurts to look at someone's bloodied mouth when it is talking and thickened red dribbles out or maybe a tooth—listening to my husband also hurt in the same way that I can barely look at a person with any kind of tumor growing on their face, an ear folded under a pus-filled bulb or a nose swollen into a rubber ball, and this is why it took all the energy I had just to listen to him talk to me in his crooked voice, that voice that sounded wrenched out of his mouth, like a molar being slowly twisted from gums with the nerves dangling, but, *Hello*, he said, and *How are you?* he said, and I said, *Good*, and we knew that wasn't really true and he said, *I'm good, too*, even though it was also obvious he was not good or even close, but regardless of all that ungoodness he talked for a while and I made some noises equivalent to an absently nodding head, but after a few minutes of this he asked, *Are you even listening to me? It's been months and can't you even listen to me? Is that so much to ask? Is it so much to ask you just to fucking listen to me for once?* And I knew listening to him was important, so I tried my best to listen, to take his words in and fold them in the correct fashion, to make a smooth, warm stack of his words, a just-laundered-white-socks-and-white-towels kind of stack, a bleached-and-tumble-dried stack that I could look at and say, yes, I had completed this chore, this thing of life that needed doing: hearing my husband's complaints, his current ones. So I let it be painful; I let the hurting just be a thing that was there instead of a thing I was feeling. I told my husband, *It's just a lot, to listen, to hear you right now. I am—I am overwhelmed, a little. I am a little overwhelmed.* And my husband said, *Yes, I understand that,* but I don't think he did understand it or even that it could be understood, what my life was like at that point and why it was overwhelming me. The moss-green hospital room and the locked door and a person from the embassy telling me I was illegal and needed to be psychologically assessed and that little painting of the man who owned the ocean reminding me that I didn't own anything at all just then, not even the freedom I'd once had and not even a glass of ocean water and here was my husband's voice asking if I was being treated well, if the immigration officers were being fair and decent and if the nurses and doctors were being kind and polite and I wanted to answer him with something true, to tell him something specific so he would know that I was

listening and answering, making a real effort, and as I
thought of what to say I looked through the narrow
window in the locked door and saw a nurse put her
hand on her lower back, twist so slightly to the right,
and the way she did this reminded me of the tender
tender at the bar on the ferry from Picton to Wellington and how the tender tender had been so very tender in the way she had slid cold pints into everyone's
hands and how her movements, pulling on the taps,
turning on tiptoe back toward me, the straight-backed
grace she had as she leaned down to rest her head in
beer-wet hands, and I thought of that tender tender
and the possible world that she had suggested just by
existing the way that she had, the possible life she had
hinted toward, and there was a glimmer of the tender
tender in the nurse as she pressed her spread fingers
against her back and because of this balmy memory I
felt a passing *niceness*, and I told my husband they
were treating me *very well* at the hospital, that everyone here was being *professional and kind*, though, in
fact, no one had treated me at all yet and I had only
spoken to that nurse with the phone and Mrs. Harper
from the embassy, who hadn't been particularly kind
but at least had seemed, in a way, professional, since
her profession seemed to be making people aware of
the bad things that they had done. My husband apologized for having to make me go through with the
assessment, but it seemed to him that this would be
the only way for my return to be a safe one, telling
the immigration officers that I was potentially a risk
to myself and others was the only safe thing for me,

and he knew, he said, that I wasn't within myself anymore and I needed to be found, but, he said, *I know you're not really a risk to yourself or others, Elly, I know that you're not, you know—dangerous—you know that, right?* That is what he actually, honestly asked me: if I knew that he knew that I wasn't a *risk to myself or others*, which, I believed, overlooked the fact that I had been locked in a small, green hospital room and told I needed a psychological assessment, that I was a highly suspect person and that I would need to be mentally and emotionally assessed, that an inventory needed to be taken because they weren't entirely sure if everything that was supposed to be in me was still in me, and all this was telling me in many ways that I was, in fact, a risk of some sort, that I had been putting a part of my life or the lives of others at risk because immigration officers don't go locking unrisky people into hospital rooms and mental health assessments are not conducted on those who are just calm, sweet darling things and *These are not the things we do to people who are not a risk to something, Husband,* I thought but did not say. I was a risk. And my husband knew that. And he also knew that I knew that. I knew, also, I was a risk to *his* life, and even though I wanted to ask him if he knew that, I didn't ask him that because I already knew the answer, regardless of what he would say, so I breathed in as best as I could and I tried to keep listening to my husband's crooked, tumor-y, pus-filled, and nearly bursting voice. And I did not want to admit this then but I can admit it now and will: I wanted to be responsible for destroy-

ing a small-to-medium-sized part of him, and this
was a somewhat-sick and somewhat-normal thing, I
think, everyone wants to feel like they *could* destroy a
small-to-medium-to-large part of someone who loves
them, though not everyone can see that ugly want
sleeping under the blankets of love and affection and
secure attachment that we try to smother that ugly
want with and even fewer people will allow that want
to become an action, to take any kind of pleasure in
seeing the destroying done. Everyone wants to be
needed so badly that if we were to withhold ourselves
from that person who needs us so, we would leave
them so empty of their need they'd become completely irrelevant to the world, unable to go on in a
normal, functional, just-fine, forward-moving fashion, and the short of it was this: my husband was a
mess, and even though I knew I was also a mess, I
also knew he was messier, at least in some ways,
and I realized I no longer had any interest in taking
responsibility for him, the crumple and grunt of
him, my husband, this life I had wedded and welded
myself to—he and the way he was and the way he
wanted me to be. My husband said something to me
about the poor choices I had made but I already knew
that I had made a poor choice or series of choices.
My choices were poor, they were broke, they were
bankrupt of all value to other people. My choices
were only of any value to me and that value, I was
coming to find, was also highly debatable, now that
I was sitting stiff and still dressed on a hospital bed,
waiting for someone to fully analyze my internal,

unseeable being and I knew so certainly they would just say what I already knew—that there had been no discernible or obvious reason behind anything that I had done—leaving my husband without a word and wandering this country for so long. I was just out here, all huddled in my nothing. I could only explain all my poor choices by saying that I had a general feeling of needing to leave, of needing to be the first to go, of needing to barricade myself from living life the way everyone else seemed to be living it, the way that seemed obvious, intuitive, clear and easy, and easy and clear to everyone who was not me, to everyone who was on the other side of this place called I.

Nothing is clear or easy to me anymore, I said to my husband, and he told me, still in that malformed voice, that he had something important to tell me. He said he would leave a letter with the doorman of his (not our) building, and that letter would tell me what I was supposed to do, it would outline what remained of the life I'd left, and what of it I could still claim. He breathed in and balanced his voice on what seemed to be the last stable edge of himself.

Elly, I am not yet sure what to do with you or myself, if there is still a context in which we can exist. You have complicated all the contexts in which we had formerly existed, Elyria, you have tested their outer reaches. There are limits to what a man can stand, to how much being treated unlike a husband he can take before he is, in fact, no longer a husband, no longer willing to be the half of the life that he had thought he was living in.

I was listening to him as carefully as I could, still taking his words into my hands and folding them into smooth rectangles and putting them in a neat stack beside me. And now my husband had told me what my next chore would be, that after I was sent back to New York there would be this letter and that seemed nice, having instructions, directions, maybe even a list with open boxes for checking and I could go check, check, check, done, done, done, and be back in my life or its vague approximation. After he told me about the letter he said that he couldn't talk anymore because he needed to go, but it was clear in the way that he spoke that he didn't actually need to, he just wanted to, though I may not be the kind of person who can be relied upon to make a distinction between wants and needs, and I may not be a person who can parse any space between needing and wanting or even wanting and being compelled or being compelled and being swallowed whole by something, picked up and taken away by something like a desire, something like a need, something like a compulsion. But I knew that what my husband meant when he said that he needed to go was that he wanted to hang up the phone and pour himself a glass of gin if the hour was appropriate or even if the hour was inappropriate and he wanted to go sit in his chair, his favorite chair   the beige one with the stain on the left arm—and he wanted to put on one of his mother's records, that unlabeled one that he'd never heard when he was a child but it was still one that she had owned, had probably paid money for or was given at some point, this recording

of a string quartet performing something just morose
enough for everyday listening, and the composer had
always been unknown because the tune was unfamiliar and the original sleeve had been lost and replaced
by a fold of plain cardboard, and as he sat in his chair
and listened to this record for the thousandth time as
he held the night's first glass of gin, he would keep the
tempo of the quartet by swinging his head so slightly
to the right (with his eyes closed), then back to center,
then throw his chin up (still with his eyes closed), then
back to center and to the right again, center, and up
again, center, eyes closed and right, center, and up,
center, still with shut eyes and right, center, up, center,
and he would do this for hours, eyes always closed,
as the record played and ended, and he'd turn it to the
B side then to the A side again and the B and the A
and this, I knew, was what he meant by *I need to go,
Elyria*; he meant he had to go into the place where he
went when I became too much for him, the place where
he conducted music played by men or women who
were (maybe) long-since dead, men or women who
he'd only known as violins, a viola, a cello, men or
women who had therefore, essentially, always been
dead to him, alive only in the recorded shadow of
once-vibrating strings, alive only when the record
spun, but somehow his mother was in that record, I
knew, and that's why he had to play it, that's why he
had to conduct it, that's why he had to be a conduc-
tor to that music, that energy, her energy, that last
crackly, rotating bit of his mother that existed and
my husband conducted those songs, also, because I

was too much for him to conduct and for that I would like to apologize, that I had always been the wrong watt for my husband, that I was always tripping his circuit, that I was never something he could quite carry.

The nurse took the cordless phone out of my hand and walked out without any kind of explanation and the door audibly locked behind her and I was just left with myself behind that locked door and even though this wasn't a particularly nice place that I was in, I decided or perhaps just felt then that I wanted this exact moment to stay awhile longer than any other moment. I said to myself, *Moment, you should stay, you should stay even though I know you can't and wouldn't even if you could,* and I wanted this, I now realize, because I loved the limits I had in that moment—the edges of my hospital bed and the hideous walls of that room and the door and the lock in the door and the country that was keeping me and the knowledge that a psychiatrist was steadily marching toward me, that he was going to ask me questions and record my answers and he was going to watch how my eyes moved and when and watch where I put my hands and how, and all these little things were going to be recorded, flattened out onto a sheet of paper that would tell the embassy and the immigration agents and Homeland Security and my waiting husband exactly what I was and why I was what I was, and I loved that these were the cozy limits of my little life, in the limit of this moment, in the antiseptic huddle of the hospital room, in the blurry cocoon around me that everyone was

calling the world, this moment—well, I wanted it to
stay, just like that April day, the first spring since
Ruby had split herself open on the brick courtyard,
and the first spring since I had met the professor who
would become my husband, when he and I were in a
park, lying on a quilt he told me his mother had made
and for the first time since I'd met him he smiled
when he talked about his mother, and the professor
and I were in the park and lying on our sides on that
quilt and holding hands and looking in each other's
eyes and both of our hearts were making themselves
known to us as highly functional organs—beating
like the strongest and most patriotic of soldiers lead-
ing the march of our little lives—and so the professor
and I were the most in love that two people could
ever be because we had been united by the loss we
had in common and despite this or because of this we
had allowed ourselves to fall in love during that all-
time darkest autumn, but then the snow had come
and gone and the ground had dried and trees had
leaves again and we were finally there in the middle of
it again, staring at the impossibility of spring, again it
was spring, and staring at the impossibility of being so
alive and being so awake with someone else and the
professor, staring at me in this yellow moment, decided to say something someone long dead had said
or written: he said, *Moment, stay*; and I said, *What?*,
and he said, *It's something Virginia Woolf wrote: Moment,
stay because you are so fair, or something like that*, and I
said, *So this is how you feel? How Virginia Woolf already
felt?*, and he said, *Yes*, and what I felt then was par-

tially agreement with him because, yes, I was also in love and wanted to stay in it, but also a kind of sadness, a kind of anger, a kind of disappointment, because as soon as he had asked that moment to stay, it was gone.

36

Here's the thing, I said to the memory of my husband, that hologram—here is the thing:

We don't get to stay in moments and that should not be news to you. We are both familiar with the concept of time, the awful math of it, how our history always gets larger, less understandable, overweight, overworked, over and over, and memories get misfiled and complicate feelings for no good reason and some people seem more able to deal with this, to keep their histories clean and well ordered but I still don't understand why we came unstuck from those moments we wanted to stay and why the moments we wanted to forget still haunt us.

Maybe it's a kind of math we can't do, something we failed, and when I think about you now I can't think about you straight—it's like you've turned into a color or a sound, like a whole orchestra warming up with the first violin doing one thing and second violin doing another and violin five doing whatever and violin seven doing nothing and cellos and drums and flutes all scribbling, no harmony, no pattern, no sense, no order. I don't even know what I'm talking about or thinking about or whether I am talking or thinking, and maybe if I was a sound or a color I wouldn't be a sound or a color, I'd be a wildebeest except that's not true because I am a wildebeest. I am part wildebeest. Of course you'd say, *That's not true, you're not a wildebeest*, and you'd try to console me: *We all have darkness*, you'd say; but I know mine is darker and that it hides a whole herd of rabid wildebeests and I'm not like you, Husband, there's no light switch in my darkness because my darkness is a midnight savanna on a moonless, starless night and all my wildebeests are running at a full, dumb speed but I couldn't even tell you this if I tried because we haven't really spoken in years, which is why I have put a distance of space and time between us, to make our silence make sense. Even if you picked up this unwritten letter and read it you couldn't actually read it because it doesn't exist because the wildebeests ate it and I'm sorry, but I'd still like to know:

Are you sleeping these nights?

Is your life livable?

Do you eat—do you eat anything at all?

Do you believe anyone cares if you are alive at the end of the day?

And where did our want go?

And who set fire to our wanting?

And who invented want and why?

Let me say that whoever invented wanting, whoever came up with desire, whoever had the first one and let us all catch it like a hot-pink plague, I would like to tell that person that it wasn't fair of him or her to unleash such a thing upon the world without leaving us a warranty or at the very least an instruction manual about how to manage, how to live with, how to understand this thing that can happen in a person against her will, by which I mean desire and the need it gnaws in us and the shadow it leaves when it's gone. And, yes, I know that this will always be our intolerable problem, one of those things we slowly go grey over, so forget it—forget what I was asking or saying and let me just ask you this: If you could hire a think tank to figure out what happened to us, would you do it? You'd think after all these months I've spent thinking about what we were and what we became that I'd have some kind of clue but I don't have any. Do you have one? Could I see it? Could I borrow it? Or is this the kind of game where you keep all the clues to yourself until the game is over and someone opens the envelope and it says: *It was the husband, in the office, with the chalkboard* (which is funny because we were all so sure that it was the wife, in the kitchen, with the chef's knife).

Sometimes I remember that afternoon you asked me to teach you how to hold a baby and put it into a crib because you didn't know how to do this and I did know and you thought that you'd someday need this knowledge, this tiny skill, and even though I knew you'd most likely never need to know how, I still taught you.

You place a baby the same way you place a blame: put it down slowly—after careful deliberation—of where to place it—and cradle the head—and mind the neck.

37

Another nurse came in and recorded my temperature, blood pressure, and heart rate and she seemed unimpressed with the way my heart was flexing and the numbers on the thermometer. She put a wooden plank on my tongue, peered into my throat, removed the plank, and tossed it into the trash. She shined a little light in my eyes and into my ears and up my nostrils, again seeming annoyed when she found nothing of consequence in me.

Time to change this, too, isn't it?

She started unwrapping the gauze and it appeared gradually more red than white and she peeled back a long flap of blood-soaked cotton. A slimy, red wound dimpled the center of my forearm. She sopped up streaks of blood, then said, *This is going to sting a little,* and poured something into that red dimple which fizzed, but I didn't feel it. She held my wrist as she wiped off the underside of the wound then rewrapped the whole thing.

There we go, she said, smiling. She made eye contact for longer than I felt was natural or appropriate. *You're lucky—a couple millimeters one way and you would have bled to death.*

She said the psychiatrist would be in soon and I tried to retain some dignity even though she knew that it had become necessary to have a psychiatrist come to assess my mental situation, but then I remembered that I didn't have any dignity to retain, not since she had measured my heart and seen all my bleeding and examined every entry there was into the slimy middle of my skull.

Later the psychiatrist showed up: a bald man with delicate, wire-frame glasses pinched low on his bulbous nose, a thin bird on a thick gnarl. He wore a lighter grey shirt under a darker grey cardigan, and darker grey pants. He had little wisps of pale hair hanging off the sides of his head, the last spring leaves of him.

It's often better if we're on a first-name basis, Elyria. Is it all right if I call you Elyria?

Sure, I said, thinking of how I'd always be sitting under that word, my name, the terminal noise of me.

My name is Thomas.

He didn't have a nice-to-meet-you look on his face but something more like a jeweler looking for authenticity.

First, Elyria—and I hope you don't take this too personally—I will need to assess your intellectual ability. This is merely a formality to confirm you are fit to complete the next survey I'll administer about how you've been feeling lately. Are you ready for part one?

I sat up a little, tried to make myself look kind and safe and trustworthy, a Labrador of a person. I said,

I'm ready, and he gave me a short, yellow pencil and a clipboard pinching one sheet of paper with math and logic problems.

Please take as long as you need, Elyria. There's no rush.

The assessment was just a few basic math problems like *nine divided by three* and *four times five* and other lines like this, problems that weren't really problems at all, problems that were so simple they made my life problems seem unbearably complex. There were a few picture ones, too: *A fish, a dog, a hammer—which does not belong? An apple, a tree, a helicopter—which does not belong?* Still, I answered them all slowly, deliberately, making sure to match the seriousness with which this test had been given to me. All moments forever had led me to this moment with these equations and this drawing of a happy, slobbering dog, knowing the answers instantly, looking at the problems again, knowing the same answers, reading them again and trying to imagine if there was any possible way that I might be wrong, but each time I always came back to my first thought and after I had written my nine answers to the nine problems I felt a little exuberance because I knew at least nine things in this world to be just so plainly true, limbless facts. I wished, for a moment, that I had become a mathematician or an accountant or a factory worker so I could just have part of my day be full of NO or YES, ONE MILLION or TWO MILLION, or SAME, SAME, SAME, SAME. But instead I had this life that was populated with so many MAYBEs or

ALMOSTs or PERHAPSes or I DON'T KNOWs
that I felt that I was swimming or drowning or boiling
in them, but here, in this quiet moment when I had
finished the intellectual assessment but had not yet
handed it back I tried to flatten my life out into a
similar format:

Husband times silence equals another country.

Ruby times brick courtyard equals negative Ruby.

Seashore, sister, seagull—which does not belong?

But my life, anyone's life, any life like a real life,
any life that is humanlike—it can't be turned into
questions like that. I handed the clipboard back to
Thomas and he looked down at it and moved a finger
down the right side of the paper, pausing for a second
on each number and letter and he nodded and looked
at me.

All right, that wasn't so bad, now was it?

No, I said. (Was I supposed to answer that question? It was not clear.)

Thomas smiled a mouthful of tiny teeth and took
off his glasses.

And how are you feeling today, Elyria?

I took a quick inventory of myself and found that
everything was here and in more or less working
order. My brain was functioning. My body was not
crushed into a pudding. And, yes, I was somewhat
trapped in this hospital room with my arm under all
this gauze and all these painkillers in my veins, but that
was, in its own way, somewhat enjoyable even though
I had so many complicated and not-completely-all-
right feelings under that enjoyment—because I knew

I was enjoying something that I also knew, on some level, was just not meant to be enjoyed—

Fine, I said. *I'm okay.*

Just okay?

Yep. Fine.

Good, good. That's good. So you're not in too much pain.

I nodded.

The nurses here are quite nice, aren't they?

Sure.

So, Elyria, let me just confirm a few things with you. I've been given a bit of information and I just want to confirm that it's all correct. Tell me if anything sounds incorrect, all right?

Okay.

You earned a bachelor's degree from Barnard. You've been employed as a staff writer for CBS for five years. You married Charles Riley, six years ago. You've had no major health problems. You're not in any debt. You've always filed your taxes on time. You were not taking any prescribed medications before you left the States. You lived on the Upper West Side of Manhattan in a building owned by Columbia University where your husband earned tenure a year ago as an associate professor in the mathematics department. Is this all correct?

Yes. It sounds right.

Now, you see, Elyria, what I just described sounds like a pretty decent life you had going on there, so you can see how other people might be confused about why you decided to just pick up and leave like you did without even telling your husband where you went. That's rather odd, isn't it?

I looked at him as if he was some object in a museum that I was not particularly interested in.

It's confusing to people, Thomas said, *why you might just get up and leave everything.*

Yes, I said, nodding and smiling just a little. *I know.*

Elyria, are you trying to avoid talking about why you left?

No.

No?

I don't have anything to say about it.

You're putting up quite a resistance to talking about it, though. Why is that?

I don't know.

You don't need to have your guard up, Elyria.

I don't have a guard up.

You seem a little guarded.

No, I don't.

How do you deal with stress?

I don't know. I read, I guess. Something alone.

Can you tell me a little more about that?

I don't really have anything to add to it. Stress is stress. You just deal with it.

I box, sometimes, to relieve stress. It feels good to hit things sometimes, you know? We all have a little anger to let out.

Okay.

So, do you do anything like that? Is there anything that's like boxing to you?

No. I'd just rather be alone.

Thomas made a few notes and I wondered if he was waiting for me to confess something strange, to say, *Yes, Thomas, in fact I like to kill whole forests of small animals to relieve stress; that's a lot like boxing I suppose, Thomas, you see—you and I are not so dissimilar from each other, now are we?* I made my face smile a little, like I was calm, like I was fine.

Do you miss your husband?

I don't think about it all that much.

So it's the same as stress relief for you: isolation. You isolate to avoid missing him.

No.

What is it then?

I just don't miss him.

Did it occur to you that you should have told your husband where you were going?

I don't remember.

What would it be like if you returned to your husband?

The same, I guess.

What do you mean by that?

We would just go to our jobs and live in our apartment and all the same stuff we used to do.

Did your husband ever do you any harm when you lived with him?

No. Nothing like that, I said. But wasn't it? I asked my silent head. Wasn't it something like that? Wasn't there something so brutal about our silences, something so acidic, something mutually abusive about the way we just had our lives so silently folded together? *No, it was nothing like that. Nothing like that.* But wasn't it something like brutality, like congealed blood, like a bruised face, a broken limb that won't heal—wasn't it *something* like that because it was in his sleep that the silent violence between us was finally cut loose, the want we had to destroy ourselves or each other came out then, a pot of soup left to boil too long, bubbling over, scorching the pot, filling the house with smoke.

Did he abuse you emotionally?

I thought for a second and said, *I don't know.*

I thought of the little redhead girl from the bus months earlier and I wondered what had happened to her and what she had meant by saying she was from a nebula and I wondered if she was all right and I wondered if I had misremembered this and she had never said such a thing and maybe that was why I was here, because I had seen so many mirages and believed them to be true and people had noticed, maybe, people had seen me standing shoeless in sheep meadows talking to no one, maybe, looking into no one's eyes, listening to nothing and answering it and isn't that the thing about these kinds of things: you never know for sure if what you see and hear is what other people see and hear, and Thomas stepped into my thought—

Did he abuse you physically?

And I wondered why I couldn't just say, *No, he did not abuse me, my husband did not abuse me*, and move on to the next question. Maybe it was because we both knew that nearly a majority of women had been, most likely, abused or assaulted or molested or whatever, and any woman who had not yet been abused or assaulted or molested or whatever should just wait, just give it a day or a year or a week or so because most likely it was going to happen to her, yes, one day she would wake up and think it was a day like any other day and by the time she fell asleep it wouldn't be that kind of day anymore, and if this never happened, if she somehow was still a member of the unabused, unassaulted, unmolested few, then she should always remember that hands that could and would assault a woman were prevalent and nearly unavoidable. There was a sense of *not if but when*, and I felt that sense while Thomas looked at me, expecting, it seemed, for me to say, *He did—I was—this is why I left, I am one of those women who can do nothing but run*, but I knew so surely, or at least almost surely, that my husband didn't or almost didn't or didn't quite, didn't really, didn't consciously, but I almost wished that he had abused me—abused me in a waking, daylight, intentional way—so that my leaving would make a little more sense to myself and the rest of the world.

Did he abuse you physically?

My mouth wouldn't let my brain move it.

Elyria, I cannot take your lack of explanation as an explanation, you know. I must only report what you confirm to be the truth or tell me is the truth. If you cannot say or confirm that your husband abused you or did not abuse you, I cannot just take what I believe you may be implying by your silence and put that down. I can only write down that you refused to answer the question, do you understand?

Yes.

Perhaps we should just come back to that one later—

I sat up and again looked at the picture of the man who owned the ocean and wished I could please become him now, pinch my nose, close my eyes, and jump into some other life.

I thought of my husband sitting in his chair, his legs crossed, his arms crossed, his voice saying, *Typical, Elyria. It's incredible how much you can forget.* Over the years there had often been things that I would forget and he would remember, memories and information that my husband had archived—things I had done, he had done, words I had said, he had said, verbatim sentences he could remember spoken by himself or others or me, things we'd seen or done or places we'd been, verbatim places, verbatim people, exactly precisely factually factual things he could remember that I could not or could not quite, completely, remember. So my husband was this constant fact-checker of my life and the idea of him making things up, intentionally or not, had occurred to me, that maybe many of the things he had told me had happened, had, perhaps, never happened—

Elyria, when did it occur to you that you wanted to leave your husband?

I don't remember, I said, and my voice did not sound true even to myself because I did remember the day I decided to leave, a Tuesday afternoon walking down Broadway—I watched an old woman in a crosswalk and I knew.

Thomas inhaled and flipped through a few pages on his clipboard.

Do you ever have thoughts about harming your husband?

No.

Harming others?

No.

Do you ever think about harming yourself?

No.

Do you ever think of suicide?

Memories sometimes move into a word or a phrase and you'll never think of that word or phrase or that feeling or color without thinking of the other side, the things you store in it, and under the word *suicide* was a cave called Ruby, and it had become impossible for me to tell anyone what I thought of when I thought of the word *suicide* because so many thoughts lit up in my brain, lifetimes of thought, and anytime I heard that word I always remembered the end of Ruby, the little knot tied at the end of us. But this, I knew, was not what Thomas meant, when he asked me if I ever thought of suicide.

So I said, No, without pausing.

Elyria, I'd like to now begin another assessment. Please answer the questions as fully as you can, all right? Okay. Are you experiencing problems with falling or staying asleep?

No.

Do you ever feel frightened or uneasy for no discernible reason?

Sometimes.

How often?

I don't know how often. Doesn't everyone feel like that sometimes?

Are you having trouble concentrating?

On what?

On anything.

Sure.

Thomas waited for me to continue, to explain my-self, but I didn't want to look back at him or explain myself because I knew that everyone who was alive had trouble concentrating on life and I knew that he, somewhere in him, knew that, too, that really being alive, being pushed around the world by whatever was in your brain, and having feet, walking on your feet, having a freedom that is always limited to how free your body is, all that was too much to concentrate on and so no one concentrated on it too often or too easily and we all have trouble concentrating on it, on everything.

Do you feel irritable or jumpy?

Both, I thought, and No, I said.

Do you feel detached or estranged from yourself and/or others?

Often, I thought, and No, I said.

Do you ever feel that you are reexperiencing a difficult part of your past?

And I thought about that sentence and the reality behind it and I thought, *Well, yes, Thomas, of course, isn't that the problem with memories, Thomas? You should know, Thomas, you're a professional in the way the mind works.* But I said, No, not really. Not that I can remember.

Has anything happened to you that you don't want to talk or think about?

What kind of question is that? I thought, and I said, *What kind of question is that?*

For instance, were there any places in New York that you found yourself unable to visit without feeling distressed?

I remembered walking long blocks just to avoid those places, distressing buildings, distressing shadows made by the light through the trees, the pinch in my throat I had when I passed the gates on the east side of the campus and that diner that had been Ruby's diner that my husband still went to some nights, where he still ate his Reubens and his spaghetti (*Who gets spaghetti at a diner?*) like nothing had happened, like Ruby had never been there, eating BLTs and staring at the cars going down Amsterdam, the sirens singing to and from the hospital.

More questions came and they melted together— *Did you experience or witness anything that was disturbing or made you afraid for your life? Any upsetting situation? When you think about the future, do you get a sense that it will be shortened for some unknown reason? Do you ever experience unwanted memories?*

And my wildebeest was telling me that all memories are unwanted, but I was saying something else, trying to give Thomas an answer that reflected my humanness and not my wildebeest and maybe also a plank of sanity, but sometimes I'd speak, stop, stare somewhere, forget what was happening, try to try to try to remember—

Elyria, we do appreciate your cooperation with the assessment, and everything will be—

I've been locked in this room for I don't even know how long—

You've been here for less than a day. You were treated

for a severe injury from a stingray and found to be overstaying your visa and now you are undergoing a psychological assessment and a post-traumatic-stress assessment. It's all very straightforward, in fact. It's all very simple.

He looked offended and annoyed. I wondered what this trauma was that I was supposedly post.

Your husband believes you may be potentially mentally unstable and we take those claims seriously. We're careful not to knowingly expose the public to someone who might not have all their wits about them—

I stared at the ceiling and knew there was nowhere I could go without being found.

Excluding your immigration status, have you been involved in any illegal activities during your time in New Zealand?

No.

Are you sure?

I'm sure, I said, but I knew I wasn't sure because memories and realities and facts and dreams had all become less distinct from one another and when I looked back on things I had done I wasn't convinced that I had done any of it and when I made a mental list of things I had not done I couldn't put anything on it and I knew the wildebeest in me was a heavy desire to destroy something without the actual ability to destroy something and maybe Thomas could also see my tiny, smiling hit man, that smug motherfucker sitting in the center of me, and in that moment I could think of all kinds of things I would rather be: a string-bean plant or a possum who just wanted to crawl and eat, instead of being a person who can't seem to find a way to comfortably live or be in this world, but I didn't want to find a way out of this life or into some other life. I didn't want to lust after anything. I didn't want to love anything. I was not a person but just some evidence of myself.

38

I was staring out my little hospital window, trying to have a significant moment, trying to realize something, to feel real. I waited, patient, but no realizations came. Nothing felt real. A deep sense of unreality came over me until, finally, a half realization came and it was this: unreality was the only reality that I had and all I could do was believe that it was enough, that unreality was close enough to reality, that reality was unreality's last name, and making do with unreality was maybe the best I could do.

I'd had a similar nonrealization of unreality before, I remembered, in the dressing room at the church where I got married, and my mother had walked in with a droop in her eyes and a curl in her voice, already sloshy before the ceremony began.

You two make a lovey brood and grime, she'd said, too proud or oblivious to correct herself. *What's the rules about the bride mother seeing the groom man? Huh? Well, I don't know what it is, but I did. I mean, your groom man. Saw him. Handsome one he is. A lovey grime, I mean—a lovey broom.*

Mostly she could keep her drunkenness a low

rumble instead of a crash and for that subtlety I was thankful, the mauve of the problem, the lovey grime. I looked at my mother and felt the jitter and pulse of her life and remembered that I had slipped into this world through her body and how that meant something, how that told me something about the kinds of accidents I was going to make because she was the only start I'd ever get.

Anyway, she said, *'stime for you to get married. Marriage! All right.*

My husband and I had decided against bridesmaids and groomsmen or, rather, had just realized we didn't know anyone who would be those people for us. The audience was just a few pews. His family and mine, terse smiles. The grandmothers were politely crying, but no one else seemed to have a feeling. His mother's absence was the largest presence, and his stepmother kept touching her hair and looking around, as if she was afraid someone might steal it off her head. My parents sat with enough space between them to put two or three children.

We said vows. An organ organed. We turned and walked out.

And as I stood in my hospital room, I tried to bring up some nice memories of my husband, to wash myself in that kind of nostalgia, in the airbrushed tenderness of memories that have been refined and pared down and shaved into almost nothing, just the image of a nice man doing something nice, detaching it from the irrevocable mess between us. Nurses came in and out of the room over the next day or so with smiles or

no smiles or news or no news or gelatinous, compart-
mentalized foodstuffs, and one nurse reminded me
that I had been lucky, so lucky that I hadn't bled to
death, but another told me my wound had never been
so serious, that it would heal just fine, and someone
read something aloud about being exported or im-
ported or deported—my removal, my soon-to-be elsewhere, and I wondered why I seemed to be having a
hard time filing my life away in an organized system,
why I was putting decades-old stories in the same fold-
ers as last week, last year, the files containing my husband shuffled in with Ruby, my father, and whomever
else, whatever else—and where did anything belong
anymore and could I ever sort myself out and if I
could, then when and how, and if I did—then what?

Someone came in with breakfast—peeled egg, leak-
ing tomato, potato tangle, butter-stamped toast—and
this must have meant that night had turned to morning again, and maybe I had slept through it or if I
hadn't slept I had at least sunk into a kind of trance,
most likely, because I didn't have a memory of opening my eyes, but it was morning and I ate the egg in a
single mouthful, yolk chalky in my throat, cheeks
crowded with soft, white shards.

Two female cops with dense hair and dense faces,
broadly drawn women, escorted me out of the hospital room and I enjoyed the walk down the hallway
and its bluish light and the way that all the nurses and
doctors tried to look at the spectacle of us without
looking at the spectacle of us, tried to see the small
woman being escorted by cops, and I loved how ugly

the light was and I loved the little flicker of eyes that I would sometimes catch and I loved that I was out of that moss-green room. And I wanted this moment to stay because I wanted to just walk and walk, flanked by two cops with a specific destination, and I wanted to just be on the way somewhere, I wanted to be on the way forever without ever getting there because that was what I really wanted, maybe, to go and go and keep leaving and leave and leave and go and leave and be going and never arrive.

I don't remember a single sound or sight of the flight, all I remember is the descent, the thud and skid of us on the runway and how, when I woke up, all the large drama of my trip now seemed small and shiny, like a collectible figurine, a pathetic chipped-horn goat made of crystal.

39

Ask Ray to take you to our storage unit in the base-ment. In a clearly marked area you'll find what is yours, including but not limited to your clothing (all laundered), your books, all the art that belonged to you, your lamps, the two chairs and one side table that belonged to Ruby, that rug you bought in Spain, your toiletries, a box of stale muesli, every bobby pin and hair elastic I could find, that licorice tea that you loved and I hated, the keys to the apartment that are now useless because I changed all the locks, and a paper bag containing all the strands of your hair combed from the carpet and fished out of the couch and swept out of corners and pulled from the bathtub drain. There is no more of you in my apartment. There is no reason for you to even take the elevator to my floor, so please do not attempt to do this. You need to take all of the boxes, all at once. I do not wish to see you. I do not wish to ever hear from or see you again. Regards.

I looked up from the letter to the doorman (not Ray, a new one) but he was watching a shoe-box-sized television and maybe he didn't know that I was an unwelcome substance in this building, that I had made my husband into a person he did not want to be, but it seemed this doorman didn't know any of this so I went to the elevator and I got off on the tenth floor like I used to do every day without thinking.

I stood at my door, now just my husband's door, and I thought about knocking and what would happen if I did and he was home and he opened his door and saw me here. He might just nod and his eyes might tremble and possibly I'd reflexively put my arms around my husband, though I wouldn't be sure if he was my husband anymore and I would press my bones against his and feel the slight slope of his waist and feel the knotted muscles on his upper back and I would notice how lightly he was holding me, as if I was covered in fine thorns.

Maybe I would let go of him and he would step away and look in my general direction but not my direct direction, not right at my absurd self, his missing wife limped home to repent. Maybe he'd have cut his hair in a new shape or maybe his eyes wouldn't be the same grassy green anymore, maybe they'd turned a hunter shade, a color used in camouflage. He'd probably stand all rigid, like he was balancing a teacup full of fire on his head, and past him I would see our living room and the window we used to smoke out of when we were younger and still in love and everything still seemed possible so we could destroy our lungs a little, we could hold fire in our fingers, dare our bodies, and past the window the light and the sky would say it might soon rain but it hadn't yet. I would want to say I was *sorry* but I would know that word was too small for what I'd done and I wasn't *sorry*, not exactly, or maybe I would generate some kind of confidence and walk into the apartment and my husband would close the front door and turn and lean back against it. I imagined that familiar thud after unlatching my backpack and I imagined what I might say right then, in that silent moment just after the thud, and maybe I'd stand up straighter and make my tired eyes more open and try to really see my husband and try to really say something to him, give him something of myself, an explanation, some balm for the burn of now, but I knew I wouldn't do any of this because there was a paralysis between us and a weariness in the way he looked at me and an unfamiliarity about his eyes—what were they anymore and why had they become this other thing?

In the present I was still standing at my husband's door, and for a moment I wondered if I was standing at the wrong door, if I was thinking of the wrong man, not a husband but some stranger, some neighbor I'd never met and I wondered how much of a difference there was between a husband and a stranger. *Stranger plus time equals husband. Husband divided by time equals stranger. Husband and wife—which does not belong? Wife plus door equals what?* But there was no equation or series of questions that could turn this moment into an answer.

To the husband mirage I said, *What if we both stayed here and said absolutely nothing to each other for a year and see how we feel after that?*

Maybe that wasn't the worst idea anyone had ever had, and maybe if we could say nothing at all for a year or some other considerable length of time, maybe that would be a way to excavate the marriage, air it out, dump it out of itself and show us if anything at all was even left in it. I imagined what that would be like, us both drinking tea or eating dinner or getting dressed or undressed or dressed again or standing, both of us, by the door putting our shoes on, but we wouldn't tick out our thoughts at the other, wouldn't need to ask the other anything, wouldn't need to keep this dialogue still running down the page of us, and most importantly we wouldn't need to feel any guilt for the silence that had grown like mold on a bathroom wall we'd sometimes halfheartedly scrub at but never commit to eradicating, because, if we had agreed to this year of silence, the mold would no longer be something we needed to clean but rather evidence of our evolution, our superiority to the basic cleanings other people had to do, almost a performance piece, that mold, that silence, a living thing we were just letting live, not something we wanted to contain or talk over or bleach dead—that mold would just be something that needed nothing, and I looked at my husband in that memory and I thought of the metaphorical mold and I knew right then there was little to nothing left between us and what had been keeping us together for so long was the rich and wild memory of how there had been so much, those past moments so nice we'd asked them to stay and now they'd all left, because moments never stay, whether or not you ask them, they do not care, no moment cares, and the ones you wish could stretch out like a hammock for you to lie in, well, those moments leave the quickest and take everything good with them, little burglars, those moments, those hours, those days you loved the most.

I kept standing there at the door thinking through all the possible ways I could make us make do with what we'd made or what I'd made, the mess, I mean, but I didn't knock on my husband's door and I wondered if it would be possible for my husband to shoot me with a microscopic bullet that would make me make sense again, a bullet that could send the proper wants through my body: the want to be in this nice apartment with this reliable, honest man who had paid bills and who came home and did the things he'd said he'd do and sometimes more, and the want to have a family because it was time for me to continue the march of people that I belonged to and this was what we had been building our life toward, my husband had once said, and I didn't know how to agree or disagree. Maybe this little bullet could also make me want to live this life that was by so many standards quite nice because we had a home and jobs and money in our bank accounts and a loaf of bread in the kitchen and good knives with sturdy handles and nice appliances and rings on our hands and we lived in a city where someone would always be willing to make you an egg sandwich despite the hour or the holiday, and we had a comfortable green couch and a record player and a decent collection of records and plenty of books and we had crown molding in our home and we had a view of treetops, and we had decently functioning bodies with lungs that could wind us and hearts pumping us and mouths that had all the regular, slimy teeth and none of the false ones, and we had genetic code that had grown us both into a respectable height and shape and I had a lot of blue dresses and black boots and he looked so nice in off-white linen shirts, as if he had been a cloud in a past life.

I should want this, I thought, but all I wanted was to wish that I even wanted to want this and if I was being honest with myself, which I sometimes was, I didn't even want to want to wish.

Look—here I am. I'm still here. I'm right where you left me, the mirage of my husband said to me in my mind.

I know, I thought.

What? the husband mirage said.

I said I know, I didn't really say, *I know you're still here.*

The letter, my husband mirage said, and I remembered the letter and how I'd been looking forward to having instructions giving me a single choice, an unmovable logic.

The mirage of my husband closed his mirage door and I stood for a moment at his real door and I knew that I knew what I should be doing and I knew how to do it and I knew it had to happen now, so I took the stairs down but stopped on the fourth-floor landing to look through the smoggy window facing the courtyard, and some amount of humanness squeezed through me and wetted my face and coursed through my body and made me shake so slightly I wondered

what my husband was doing right then and I wondered what he'd ever do now that we'd both have to
do things in this new kind of *without*, the kind of *without* that was final, the kind that meant there would be
no apologies, no forgiveness, and now we'd each have
to go about the slug of waking, bathing, eating, without the other as a witness, this person we'd split so
much of our lives with, a person who housed entire
armies of information about the other and *who*, I wondered, who would we thumb over our pasts with and
who would notice how golden my husband's pale skin
became in the lamplight in his office so late at night
when his mind would move chalk sticks across, across,
across, creating problems and solutions and problems
and solutions and if there was no one to notice these
things about my husband would my husband even exist
anymore? And where would all the me that he had
housed in himself go if I wasn't there to be with him
and see what he kept of me in him, and did the versions of each of us that we had crafted so exactly and
precisely for the other person, did those versions just
evaporate, just die, just disappear, just fall out of a
building somewhere in each of our brains and if they
did then why didn't we get to have funerals for them?
I loved the he that he was to me. I loved him and he is
dead and I want a black moment for that man. Give
me a black moment for that.

40

The doorman who'd let me slip by was gone and Ray was there as I opened the stairwell door—

Mrs. Riley, no one was 'sposed to let you up there.

Ray still had that immovable mass of black hair and the one blond eyebrow and the one set of blond eyelashes, a thing that turned this broad, dense man into a kind of puppy.

Did the new guy give the letter to you? He was 'sposed to.

Yeah, I got it, I said.

Ray got a set of keys from the desk. The little TV was still on, a weathergirl in front of a map, her arm moving in a slow karate chop.

I should take you to the basement, then. Right? Get your stuff?

Sure, I said, and I tried to smile and seem grateful.

We got into the elevator and when it opened in the basement Ray held an arm in front of the door and looked toward me to signal he was letting me off first, but he looked above my head instead of at my face and I realized Ray probably wouldn't look at me because he must have thought I was a bad thing, even though he had said *Good morning!* to me so many times and so sincerely and asked *How ya doin', Elly?* and even bothered to listen to and maybe care about how I was doing and often he had carried my groceries when I came stumbling into the lobby and once he even took the elevator with me all the way up to my apartment because I had been sick and didn't look well and Ray had noticed and done something about it and despite all that history, Ray could now not even look at me, wouldn't even just gently once look. To Ray I was just a chore now, just a thing that he had to endure; to him I had smacked the humanness from myself.

Ray stacked my boxes and two chairs and little table on a rolling pallet and pushed the pallet to the freight elevator, and in the lobby he unloaded everything from the pallet and stacked it in the vestibule beside a bench I hadn't ever noticed before, since this lobby wasn't a place where I had ever waited, just a place I had passed through in that part of the past when I knew where I was going, where I should be, and what I should do. When Ray was done he didn't say anything, just rolled the pallet away, and left me and my things like he was leaving anyone and anything and he was, because objects are just slow events and people are just slow events and Ray was done with the part of his life that I would be in and from here on out I was a stranger to him and even if I saw him on some sidewalk someday and had an impulse to say *Good morning*, he would not see me and he would not say anything and he would not look in my eyes because to him there would be nothing there to see.

I sat on the lobby's bench for a while and had no-where to go and I wondered if there was a number I could call for a Man with a Van who might double as a therapist or priest or someone who could just tell me what to do with myself, someone who could take me and my furniture and boxes of life stuff to an-other part of the world or the city and tell me what to do in it, someone who knew a wide, clear place where I could start over. I wondered if there was such a thing as a Life Re-creation Specialist but I was mostly certain that if I was to look in the yellow pages for such a thing I'd only discover that it did not or did not yet exist—it would be up to me to find a new place in the world for my self and life and it seems that everyone else who was living or dead knew that you can only make those kinds of decisions for yourself and no one else can make them for you, and that there was probably something potentially very wrong with the woman who had a hard time just choosing any-thing to do with her whole entire self.

After some time, something like an hour or hours, Ray came over and told me that I couldn't just sit in the lobby all day now that I didn't live here anymore. He generated some kind of pity and asked, *Don't you have anywhere to go?* He seemed almost sincerely con-cerned about where I could possibly ever go and I sur-prised myself when I said, *Yes, I do have somewhere to go,* and I said it in a fed-up way, and again it was my voice, not my brain or body telling me how I felt and this was news to myself because being fed up wasn't what I thought I was. *I have plenty of places to go,* I said, and I stopped looking at Ray and dug through my backpack and took only the things that were the most necessary (toothbrush, papers from immigration, little wooden camel Jaye had given me, socks, passport, underwear, a shirt) and I put them in a small canvas bag that seemed now preferable to the lug and labor of a backpack. I considered looking through the boxes for something else I might need like shoes that were more functional or clean pants but it wasn't worth the trouble of having to push past the blue dresses and think of my husband taking things off their hangers and folding them and putting them in these boxes. A happy UPS man walked into the lobby, he and his shorts and his smile and his name sewn on his shirt, and Ray chatted with him, happy to talk to someone who was who he was expected to be, who came and did and went just like that.

While Ray spoke and joked with the UPS man I walked out of the lobby and immediately regretted telling Ray that I had a place to go because, in fact, I did not have a place to go and that was exactly where I was going. I made it to the end of the block before Ray started yelling after me about all the things I'd left in his lobby, so I turned the corner onto Broadway and sprinted toward the train and I don't know if Ray was running after me or not, because I did not look because I was too busy running as a way of saying, *Fuck you, everything, fuck all of the things forever because I am free, so free,* but also I knew that I wasn't free, because running from something isn't freedom, it's just a way to flee, and, sure, the day was what a person talking to another person would call beautiful, but I immediately took it for granted, felt the earth owed me this one warm favor.

In the subway station I jumped the turnstile as if that was how I'd always gotten around and I bolted into a waiting car just as the doors closed and we went and no one cared and I looked at all the people around me, staring off, headphones plugging ears, some sleeping or almost sleeping, and no one cared—oh, how no one cared—oh, how I loved how no one cared.

Standing in front of me was a man with a bald spot, a sign I could trust this man because he, too, knew loss. I stared at his little bit of naked scalp, how tender, how shining, how close it was to his brain, his whole entire self. After some time he got off the train, so I got off the train, too, and I trailed behind the full moon his scalp was and when I lost track of him in a push of postwork people that was fine—we always knew it would end like this, that it would have to end somehow.

I watched my feet moving across the sidewalk and realized my shoes were at the brink of giving up on me and the rest of the world: the lace tips frayed, seams strained, a little mouth opening on one toe as if gasping for air or like it was trying to whisper, *Enough, enough, haven't you figured out that there is nowhere better or worse to go and other people put up with this fact and you, for some sickness, do not, and will you stop trying to see a meaning in everything, in anything, and will you stop wishing you could have come close to any sheep in New Zealand just so you could touch the animal who filled the*

world with wool and will you stop talking to your own
shoes and imagining them talking back at you? I did not
particularly like listening to my shoes speak to me.
They did not have anything useful to say.

As I walked down the West Side Highway, cars
shushing beside me like an ill ocean, I heard heavy
steps, then a man's voice—*You one sexy-ass bitch*—
spoken so low I wondered if I was supposed to hear
him or if it was a note to his sexy-ass self and then the
man was to my left, and he looked over his shoulder
at me before speeding up, his eyes scanning the crowd
ahead of him, looking for other sexy-ass bitches. On
a bench a man in ripped grey clothes with plastic bags
on his feet was asking anyone if they had fifty cents—
It's just fifty cents, it's only fifty cents—but when I passed
he stopped asking and he gave me a look I'd never gotten before and I took that look and put a frame around
it and hung it up in me. Every few minutes or so I
would remember the look from the man who had
wanted fifty cents, and I'd look at that framed memory
hanging in myself and it meant I was here, back in this
sick city, but in other ways I was not here at all and
anyone who looked closely could see that I had nothing
to give, that I was a junk drawer, a collection of things
that may or may not have had a use.

I kept wandering through all these dirty, winding
streets and all my thoughts and observations were immediately self-destructing, not a single memory made,
and then I noticed that the sky had produced clouds
that would have made a person believe in God if they
were susceptible to believing in God but all they did

to me was make me wonder if it had been a good idea
to start walking across the bridge toward Brooklyn
because it seemed that considerably less people were
out here than usual, like everyone knew something
was about to happen but I didn't and those God
clouds got fat and dark and let their rain come down
onto the bridge and the river below went stucco tex-
tured and my body and my canvas bag quickly looked
as if we'd just stepped out of the ocean, some sea
monster in the wrong place. The few others on the
bridge were smug and safe under umbrellas and it was
clearer to me than it had ever been that all there is on
earth is the eternal now and nothing else. I had heard,
in the past, lots of people say that, say that nothing
exists except the present moment, that nothing has
ever happened, that no one is here or not here, that no
object is more than its action in a moment, and if all
this business about the present moment is true, and I
am still inclined to believe that it is true, then all I
was at that moment was a set of senses held captive in
a wet body in wet clothes in the piss of a cloud, stranded
on the center of a bridge and I was just that and nothing else, and the past, the recent past, and the less
recent past were not a part of me, just something
gathered around me, an audience for what I would do
next.

The rain gave up and left and I wrung my hair out
over one shoulder, then found a bench on the Brooklyn end of the bridge and I tried to hug some of the
water out of my clothes and I took my shoes off and
took off my socks and twisted the rain out of them

and put them back on anyway because the other socks I'd brought with me weren't any drier and as I was doing this a woman under an umbrella walked up and held out a few tissues she'd pulled from a plastic pouch. I said thank you and she said nothing and when I took them they turned to slime, sopped with the rain on my hands. She put the whole plastic pouch on the bench beside me and walked away wordless, so I watched her go, watched all of her goodness and empathy get away from me. I wondered why my husband couldn't have just been all bad. Why couldn't he have been a cartoon villain, someone I could have fled from and known I had made the right decision? Why must there be nice memories of him sitting beside the ugly ones, both of them oblivious, strangers on a bus? And I still wanted my black moment for it all, and I was still waiting on that black moment, still felt I was owed it, a little funeral for the us we'd been. I needed to stop wanting that impossible funeral, needed to leave that want like dogs must leave what their owners tell them to leave—I was something like a dog I owned. I had to tell myself to *leave it*, to *shut up*, had to take myself on a walk and feed myself and had to stare at myself and try to figure out what myself was feeling or needing.

By the time I started walking again the sky was going dim and the air became this nice blanket tucking us in, telling us to sleep well, sleep tight. I followed a broad, busy street where the bridge ended and I almost reflexively stuck my thumb out but I got the impression that this wasn't the kind of thing a person should do in New York so I didn't. Some sirens were screaming over and over, fire trucks and police cars and ambulances, those urgent noises that remind us that someone is always burning or breaking a law or having their body give up and if it is not you yet who is burning or breaking or falling apart, then you can be sure that it soon will be, that soon the sirens will come for you but you will never be missing to yourself and all you can do is delay, delay, delay, and the delaying must be good enough for you and you must find a way to be fine with the delay because it is your whole life and the minute you really go missing is the minute you can no longer miss.

Outside a grocery store a man was handing out flyers that said *Do You Suffer from Chronic PAIN?* And the word *pain* took up a third of the page and the man was saying, *We got the best deals on massaging the deep tissue. Massage therapies. Massage therapies.* I passed him quickly and when he tried to hand me a flyer I pretended as if I couldn't see him even though he was impossible to ignore, this huge, pale man wearing an orange traffic vest, a wild grey-and-white beard, thick glasses. *Are you in pain?* he asked and I smiled. It made me smile. I don't know why it made me smile.

The sun was all gone now, the city left to light itself. I walked through a dark neighborhood with narrow streets and wide trees. I walked behind a tall, dense man who walked as if he was the president of a country called Life and it seemed to me that if I could be associated with him, somehow, I would be safe, so I followed him without wondering where he might be going, followed him like baby ducks will follow any-thing that will lead them, an alligator, a small goat, an electric toy car. I dreaded the moment he would go inside his house or any other place he might go where I couldn't, but that never happened because after I had followed him a mile or so he stopped and turned and said, *Who the fuck you doing this for?*

My voice was an ice cube stuck in my throat. I waited. We stared. It melted. I said, *No one.*

The fuck you are. You following me, bitch? You think you're just going to follow me?

I don't know where I am going, I said and I was shak-ing and he was the opposite of shaking and he took a step back, inhaled slow, and I saw a diner across the street, a twenty-four-hour sign beaming and I decided to cross the middle of the street and just leave him alone because he now seemed to not be a good person for me to be following.

You tell your man I had enough of his shit, he yelled. *I had enough, you got me?*

Okay, I said, but I said it so quietly that no one could hear it but me.

If I see your fucking face again, it's gonna be personal, he said, his voice getting softer, getting personal. *You tell your man. You tell him that.*

So I did—I invented a little man in my head and I told him, *It's going to be personal.* I think he understood. Everything is personal.

Not many people were in the diner and a waitress smiled at me in a way I had not seen anyone smile in a long time and she said, *Sit wherever you like, I'll be with you in just a minute.* I ordered a plate of something that came with everything and when *HELLO My name is BELINDA* asked me if she could bring me anything else I said, *Yes,* and she said, *What's that?* And I said, *What?* And she said, *Anything else?* And I thought for a second and said, *Coffee,* and this seemed to explain something to her, this desire for a cup of coffee at some hour that must have been close to midnight, and so BELINDA smiled and said, *All right, sweetie.*

I spent the next memorable portion of my life watching the rippled surface of my coffee quiver and I knew with an increasing intensity that everyone on this planet is also always shaking ever so slightly all the time, that the earth shakes us by shifting and settling its stone self, and the machines we've made, they also shake us, the air conditioners and eighteen-wheelers and marriages and electric generators and the people who dance with so much stomping and the wrecking balls and the bulldozers and the cars that go so fast and hit other cars and animals and the radio signals and the lives around us that run at a frequency that interferes with our own frequencies. We do not notice any of this shaking until we do notice but most people will be able to forget it for a while until they notice again but I cannot stop seeing how the earth and everything on it is ever and ever shaking, all the time, the plant stems breaking through the sidewalk and the steel beams and the skyscrapers and the people who think they are sitting perfectly still, and I can't seem to stop seeing everything quivering all the time, husbands sitting in armchairs and chalkboards and brick courtyards and the tops of trees you can see from the windows and good knives and linen shirts, and being unable to unsee the little shake that is everywhere has made it too difficult for me to go about life in the way that other people seem to be able to go about it, people ordering lunch in a deli and old ladies wearing too many coats and the policemen on smoke breaks and teenagers with secrets and smiles and the birds that just fly and are, and the leashed dogs, walking leashed in the streets, tethered to their owners, happily tethered forever. No one is anything more than a slow event and I knew I was not a woman but a series of movements, not a life, but a shake, and this put a knot in my throat and a pause in my breathing and it turned my stomach, to know that my stomach was not a stomach but a turn and my breath was nothing if it did not move and my throat without my voice was just some slowly decaying meat but I had nothing to say anymore, not yet, and BELINDA refilled my coffee and the surface rolled and rippled and then it almost stilled but not quite because it shook as it will always shake and I watched it keep shaking.

ACKNOWLEDGMENTS

Deepest thanks to Jin Auh, Eric Chinski, Emily Bell, and everyone at FSG and the Wylie Agency who helped turn this manuscript into a book. I'm also grateful to the editors who encouraged and published early excerpts: Cal Morgan at Harper Perennial; Dave Eggers, Chelsea Hogue, and Jordan Bass at *McSweeney's Quarterly*; Alban Fisher at *trnsfr*; Brandon Hobson at *elimae*; Natalie Eilbert and Jillian Kuzma at *The Atlas Review*. I am forever humbled and grateful for the support the New York Foundation for the Arts offered me during the completion of this work.

These fine people—Sean Brennan, Kendra Grant Malone, Danny Wallace, Sara Richardson, Sasha Fletcher, Peter Musante, Summer Shapiro, and Filip Tejchman—need to be thanked for so many things in the past, present, and future. And, for lovingly tolerating the writer at your dinner table, a sort of entertaining misfortune, I'd like to offer a grateful apology to my family—blood, lagniappe, and chosen—especially to my past and present collaborators at 3B, who helped me build a room of my own.

Keep in touch with
Granta Books:

Visit grantabooks.com to discover more.

GRANTA